THE KILCOLMAN NOTEBOOK

Brandon Originals

The **Kilcolman** Notebook

Robert Welch

First published in 1994 by
Brandon Book Publishers Ltd.
Dingle, Co. Kerry, Ireland

British Library Cataloguing in Publication Data is
available for this book.

ISBN 0 86322 180 7

This book is published with the financial assistance of
the Arts Council/An Chomhairle Ealaíon, Ireland

Front cover painting: *Elizabeth I* by John Bettes,
reproduced by permission of the National Maritime
Museum, Greenwich, England.

Typeset by Koinonia Ltd, Bury
Cover design by The Graphiconies, Dublin
Printed by ColourBooks Ltd, Dublin

For Seamus Heaney

I

TODAY I CAME through Buttevant's ragged ruins. Dismay is what I feel when I'm there. The pointlessness of those places. But then I remember that I am someone constitutionally given to the cultivation of misery; a fabulist of my own distresses; fabling, fabling images all the time for this condition. Contempt is the emotion to which my temperament most inclines, contempt and its ally, adoration. Give me a chance and I will be cynical and adulatory at once. Knowing and innocent.

Again now I'm confronted with the undersea shelf of myself. A great blackness. A silence. And again here I am trying to question this blackness in these private records, unofficial voicings, where I plumb bafflement: a knight wearing the insignia I came upon in those dreams that must at some stage form part of this record – a red cross; a fish of iron; the hermaphrodite.

My official stories – they are before the world, and while they are not adulated, are admired. My themes are all fairly standard: the Queen's doings; the predominance of love; the need for caution in the affairs of state. When I think of this work I cannot help feeling that dismay typified for me in the ruins of Buttevant. My pleasure resides in the fact that even when I am conducting the story along all the official lines I am also attempting to interrogate them, by introducing an element of sheer illogic. For example, in my latest piece on queenly chastity, I have a dwarf lying under the bed of state, weeping at the slight weight of the virgin body over him. He appears later in the story looking through a window as a man of arms is baring a girl's posterior. I call him Anus. And even as I write this now I am sickened by the thought of this ludicrous prank; but I am compelled into this faithlessness by a viciousness in my temperament, which delights in fragments.

And what am I doing, a family man (whose chief delight is, when fully at peace, to sit by the fire with the youngest one, listening to his soft babblings, as he tries to talk, all my heart ablaze with tenderness) doing, fragmenting thus? There is an argument that the images we generate pass through us and do not affect the nervous system, but this is something I could never accept. I know it to be a fact that the images we see and make others see affect the conduct of our inner lives, generating further images and stories of their own kind. The only way this can be checked, it sometimes seems, is to provide extensive keys to the pictures that arise, with elaborate explications. Then anything that enters the mind can be referred to its image cluster in the key and a suitable interpretation given. For example, in such a book, my dwarf, Anus, would be explained as Ireland. Or Spain. Or whatever. Small, lecherous, impotent, voyeuristic, hirsute. And so on. You can visualise his little wrinkled face, his button nose, his clouded eyes, even his speech, of which the book would give specimens. All his vocabulary would have to do with excrement. A philosopher wishing to address himself to the condition of the body politic in one of these countries (Ireland say), and eager to relate his hostility directly to the actualities of life therein, could refer to the inefficiencies of Irish sewage disposal as a way of pretending to extenuate the filth and malignity of the people of that nation, those dwarves. The like could be done with Spain, or indeed any other country. You will see that such a book would perform two very valuable social functions. It would, first, interpret the image of the dwarf looking on at the obscenity in the interior room, thereby to some extent annulling its vicious effect on the minds of the readers; and, second, it would direct the lechery aroused by the operation of the image on the mind to the beneficial end of hating those whom the tendency of public opinion at any time requires us to hate. This is a wise and judicious hermaneutic: a controlling and directing of the impulses of lust and hate, to the greater benefit of the entire system of the state, and to the profit of the hermaneut himself. A book like this, with prurient images of the most filthy kind, would sell very swiftly.

The time will come when such a writing, such excesses, will become necessary; of that I have no doubt, and it is part of my sorrow that I cannot participate in that which is yet to come. But there is the other side too, when I know that to participate in such miseries of explanation and vile satisfaction would be a diminution. I remember that my official writings sometimes seem to accord with the highest designs: the celebration of the divine ordinance of state; the perfectibility of nature in human love; the harmonious joining of heaven and earth in stanza form. When I am describing the figure of my friend Raleigh, for example, coming towards me, dressed in black, all my rhymes singing, it then seems that I have attuned my words to the exact outlines of man's destiny. Who knows what is to become of him, that man of the main-sea deep? But my stanzas discern, in the moods of their voicings, his depth, his conscience, his fate. And it is not good. Not good. I do not understand. I understand so little.

I have decided to make use of the languor of these nights in this unbuttoned form of writing. Ireland is a desert in winter. My house here at Kilcolman, with its thick walls, keeps us warm, my wife, my children and I. I, a fragmenter in love with wholeness; an Englishman in love with England, because I can discern its depth; afraid of Ireland's impenetrability. I would caress these hills around me, give them soft Latin names, but they are foreign, silent in the night around me. A shelf of blackness. My own self's dark.

II

THIS IS THE second night of these excursions that I plan. My nature does not have the flexibility of that Frenchman that one hears of, Montaigne in his tower, trying to selve himself above the fields of his estate, getting ironical. My vista is sombre, more amenable at night when I can think of the lake and Arlo's hill. In daylight they are so often bleak, but at night I seem closer to their mystery.

I am a colonist of the mind. I know this. My object, my highest desire, is to invigorate this landscape with my ecstacy, to impassionate it, to make it sing out. When I wanted to praise my awkward love from the east, my difficult shining one, I thought this location into an animation of deities, movements, voices. Places that are found in song, numbered, are never the same again, or at least that is so in England. In this country the hills are imperious, resistant to my chimings, my thinking. The water of the Mulla, even as I am thinking it now, bears only the faintest touch of the music that I made it sing for that girl from the east. Its stream is dark, its voicings those out of some impossible distance, cold remoteness, and deep as my own instinct for savagery. Today I brought Sylvanus, my son, down to the lake, to interest him in the water's movement. Why do I make these excursions?

He looked at it and said: "Father, it is so cold. Why can we not go to the city of the sun in the east that you tell me of at night? It is a cold place. Father, I am afraid. Nioclás told me that there was a monster in there, and that a man that saw it once had his face twisted all to one side. He had a name for it too; he said it was the Muirdris. Nioclás said that the man who wanted to kill it was a brave king, and he died. The blood of the Muirdris turned the water red. That is why the lake is that colour sometimes."

Fumbling now, in terror: "But Sylvanus, if the king killed the monster we now have no more to fear. You and I are safe. The king. I have heard of him. He came from across the sea, and was a brave knight wearing the red cross."

"Are you sure, Father? Nioclás said the monster comes back again forever."

"I am sure. True opposition defeats all our fears and all the fears of the deep. Opposition that is true springs from faith. As I have often told you before in our lessons together. You must strive never to forget that, Sylvanus."

He must strive. I too. I too. All my life is such; my brain a lethargy wanting not-knowing: my language wishing for silence. Until I catch a glimpse of her radiance that summons up all my wishing again, all my craving for full speech.

At the lakeside there are just my son and me and the water's reddish depth. He in whom so much of my care is vested, to whom I am so bound, at whose conception a star seared across the violet sky, and in the depth of whose eyes I can see sometimes, very far in, three girls dancing in tiny, tiny forms. A million years away and as many miles, deep down, dancing, in the fibres of his brain and flesh composed out of air and fire. Such sunlight blesses that revolution in his eyes that its white focus marks my eye with dark for many days, and I carry it with me, transferring it continually to objects and places and people, the dark of my son's light. Such a volume of depth between us I am troubled by it. And my speech gives out by the lake. I was trying to think of what I should be saying but memory went all awry, jumping from one blackness to another.

Between us both the Muirdris composing itself in silence: horny head, red eyes; rank smell from huge jaws; fetid loins, rotting in a green growth; a sack around its middle containing literature with titles like: *Calvin's cacophonies confounded; The Organ of the bishop of Rome compared with that of Elizabeth of England; Burning a man's head in three easy lessons*. Stupid inconsequences; how I lack control and order in my nature. What misery do I pass on to my children? What green stink? They are implicated, because of the water that flowed from me out to them.

III

TODAY WAS A day of silence. Much of it I spent up here in my room. It is a room that I like, being in the Irish style of masonry, in which the stones of the walls curve in, through careful placing, and with very little mortar, so as to become the roof, both side walls converging at the apex which is then surmounted by a series of triangular pieces to ensure that the water runs off down the smooth stone sides. It is an architecture for rain. The inside is remarkably dry, and here I have my writing desk of rough wood. It had to be constructed inside the room, the door being tiny.

The window is also very small, and I had it fitted with Cork glass when I took up residence. I can see through it and the view is out towards Arlo's hill. The glass being thick distorts the light, and often one of my children will swim into two segments as his image passes through a lump in the glass. Or I move my head so as to trouble the landscape with its motes.

Today I was startled out of, what shall I call it, reverie – not trance; I am only entranced when I am seeing with all the fibres – by the figure moving through the fluid medium of the window. Struggling through the irregularity in his dark clothing, he seemed like Raleigh when he came from Youghal all that time ago to take me to London. I can remember him now, that man from the main-sea deep, with those blue eyes and the laughing mouth. He was of the ocean, had a salt depth and clarity.

"Look," he was saying. "Look, man, you are a great poet. You are inflammatory. The Queen needs you, because your writing is a construction of the commonweal. You take us so far that you see our nature even as we compose it in the air we breathe. Your poetry *is* our breath. Your verse is England re-beginning. You show us what it is to conceive. Your verses are the numbering and saying of the mystery of generation and life. The Queen must love you if she loves life, if she loves herself, if she loves me. And she is most capable of love, though surrounded by scurvy knaves whose each thought is a snot. You are the high canzoneer of England. I am Ocean, and I say so. You can tell them all that you've had it out of Proteus via Walter. And, good God, what are you or I doing in this place among the loutish Irish? Manhandlers all. Offering you their women's pits, even offering to feel

15

you up themselves, and the next minute they're snarling at you with a dagger. I prefer my blackamoors black; not this dull grey in which the Irish specialise. Sperm so weak it cannot compose a lustre. A degenerate race, without speech, without love, without grace."

He could talk for hours; all his speech so crystalline, so definite. But now it is a talk underwave. A troubled monotone cast in the form of a female plaint for freedom from her undersea incarceration. She, his gentleness, crying out so thinly through the hard whorls of the rock's configurations, locked, as she is, in the structure of an undersea shelf of granite. Grey submerged eminence. Thin plaint. And above, the sea so nicely calm, or at times troubled by the adventures of the wind of which he was the past master. And why is he there now? I put him there. My stanzas have locked him in, pretending to free him, the same knight whose gentleness I undo., I, the wild one, split him into two, unmade his force; he whom I admired, and who, I think, loved me. It is not often recognised, but I am a dangerous man to be with, a bringer of discord; not a Lord of Misrule, but expert in the deep antagonism that separates us to our different coldnesses. But what choice is there for me? When I have been brought to see all that huge submarine world that is growing and extending its domination? I sing of brightness, spontaneous invigoration by water under the dazzling sunlight, earth sizzling with forms of life, birds detaching themselves from the clay to cry out notes that inspire deeper turbulences in the mud to bring out trees and flowers and perfumes that also work to bring out more; but all of this is dancing over the looming rock deep down in which poor Raleigh's girl is trapped, the girl that he is when most himself as grizzled Ocean.

I have a tale to tell of this dilemma, but later. It is to be called "The Healing", and is based on one of the dreams I had when sailing to London with Raleigh to see the publication of my long poem on *The Faerie Queene*.

When we got to Cork it was a mild windless day. Our ship was not ready to sail yet. Raleigh's eyes as we sat, drinking, were ablaze with energy.

"Cork, Spenser. The bung of Ireland. Eire's anus. Or should I say its hæmorrhoid. O noble pile, what transports do I feel when I contemplate thy oozy toil. This damn stink, Spenser, is an intoxicant. And this thick beer inflames the liver. The grave livers of Cork specialise in producing this ale to turn our livers to cork. While they, the Daneburghers, ensoul themselves in cash. This is the danegeld our Queen allows. To the greater benefit and prosperity of our most loyal and loving subjects."

"Do you think that this city can become a peaceful haven for our English merchants?"

"Your sobriety is your drunkenness, Spenser. I suppose you think that the framing of these streets in English verse, the dance of consonants along a line, will occupy the air hereafter, purifying it to the crystalline clarity of a city under imperial sway. Poets should live either in the country or at the centre, which is where you're headed now. But look, we have time to kill in this Daneburgh, and I hear the whores are clean, imported specially from Mitchelstown and Tunisia. Come on. You could do with a touch of elegant fucking after your country rutting in Kilcolman. It will clear your head for higher matters. And do not underestimate the body's trance. Sickly serious Edmundo non Mundano. Spensero pensivo. But you're a deep one, I know. You'll like the finery of Cork's sweet venery. Let go the puritanism. For once."

His chaotic words I can always recollect. It is like a mannerism that my own mind can slip into, a playfulness.

We went. Down through damp streets, savouring the rising stink of Cork's complicated waterways. It is a city built upon a series of islands around which the Lee can spread its silted flood. The river's branches are open sewers, and at high tide the smell is rank and intriguing. A damp tidal place, calling for tenaciousness in the inhabitants, a tenaciousness I can hear in the flat nasal voices of the men as they exchange ribaldries or swear at each other. The people here always seem to be shouting a parting shot.

IV

S HE WAS WEARING a tight silky cloth of gold that moved along each limb as she moved. All her movements were ravishing. I longed to make her stay in each one so I could savour it, enjoy it in full langour. A sense of her impossible beauty filled me: my erection strained and I wanted it to last for ever. Her eyes were circled with a black colouring that, she told me in response to my agitated enquiry, came from Arabia. She was not young: in her late twenties possibly, but she was perfectly made. She was English, not Irish or African.

"I think you must be one of the sly ones, Master Pensivo." (Raleigh had told her that was my name: I could hear him roaring encouragement in the next room, the

19

door of which I had asked to be closed, wishing, as always, for privacy.)

"I think you wish me to abuse you, do you not? I have much experience with men of your difficult type, scholars and courtiers. So inflamed you are. Men that are looking for the impossible. A relish for despair and all its details. I can take you very far, very far. You will not forget what I can reveal to you about disgrace. It will empower you, your abasement. We are subtle, escaping your anger that would undo us, because you hate us with every cell in your head, while at the same time longing impossibly for us. You want us to die, but I will give you that small delicious death you so crave, but not yet, not yet. I will make you spurt."

"Alice," she called out and walked to the door to the stairway, slowly, making me long to possess every fibre of her being, each curve of her buttock making me wonder at its smooth intricacy. As she moved her clothes crackled and hissed, and her walk was an avowal of the sensuality of the air itself; she made one feel as if it could caress and provoke her intimately.

"Alice," she said again, loudly. And Alice came in. She was younger, only partially clothed in very fine light stockings and shoes with stacked Venetian heels. Her mound was bare and she was caressing it as she walked.

"Come Alice. I am hot. It is irritating. Master Pensivo is hot, but we must prohibit him relief. Please release me from these clothes. My skin is so sensitive that it irks me to be much clothed. And as you remove my dress please remember to do it very slowly, so Master Pensivo gets more tense; which is what we want?"

To me this last remark. My throat was burning. Would Alice get the other girl to touch her deeply?

I asked them using exactly that phrase. It had often come to me at night sitting over Plato's text from Florence; to get one girl to touch another "deeply".

"Oh yes, but only with the small finger. I do not wish to be rudely interfered with. Alice keeps a finger especially perfumed for this most exquisite function, which I ask you please to kiss now before insertion. You must also listen very carefully to those little sounds which proceed from this most delicate ministration, that fine parting, that soft receptivity. So please observe, quietly."

All this time Raleigh was roaring next door, but in the intervals between his shouts of glee our threefold silence sank into my mind, charged with sensitivity.

Alice removed the older girl's dress. The white flesh, slightly roseate from the warmth of the fire, and mellowed by the candleglow, was supple and firm. When her dress fell about her feet Alice slowly infiltrated a tender hand into the other girl's soft underwear, an intrusion which produced a look of torture and of pleasure on the other's face. She bit her lip.

Alice removed her hand from the girl's white underwear to caress her breasts, each one full and tense, a tawny star at the tip. There were no sounds but for the sounds of their caresses and the occasional grunts from next door where the festivities seemed to have subsided. As they fondled each other they were looking at me when their eyes were not closed in real or simulated ecstasy. A terror found its way into my mind, that all of this was not sustainable. My erection, so gloriously firm, was subsiding. Phrases came into my mind; one I remember – something like *Convey hence my tristful queen*. Alice was weeping now with pleasure or with pain as the other was on her knees performing an oral manipulation, tasting the bitter secrecies. Her hands held the other's white mounds and her underclothes were halfway down her thighs. They were imprisoned in each other's caresses. My stare, so eager to begin with, was holding them, incarcerating them into maintaining the rigour of all these ceremonials.

"We are not at all done yet, Sir Pensivo," my whore was saying. "Many of our English civil servants, when they come to these shores become very inflamed. Poor creatures without the comforts of English life. One of their favourites after they have witnessed this our *tableau erotique* is to break upon our naughtiness from the other room dressed in friar's clothing. The cord, rough hempen stuff, is used then to chastise us, but the poor friar, even as he works his virtue on us, our attraction works upon his lower senses, and he finds he cannot resist our beseechingness, our soft submissions."

"These," Alice speaking now, turning coyly, stroking her smooth posteriors, "are our soft submissions."

I, too, was trapped. Who was manipulating whom? Rituals. Entrapment. Alice pointed to the corner where hung the harsh brown robe of a Franciscan. I put it on, feeling ridiculous. Someone even had taken the trouble to perfume it with incense and lavender.

"You must go through there, where your companion is,

and then come in and surprise us at our frivolities. Do not be too long. We both now desire the harshness of your male intrusion. Your tough leathern stick."

Silently and in shame I made my exit. When I entered the next room I saw Raleigh riding the fifty-year-old mistress of the house upon the dining table, dog style. Both of them were looking towards me in their labours. Raleigh's oceanic eyes were wide open, impossibly blue in the bright light of the candles which they had pushed aside. An orange rolled along the polished oak and plopped to the floor.

"Ah, good Friar Pensivo, will you shrive me timber in a minute? Indeed there is one stout club that is not Christian at all, even now being in Hell. Ouch. This, Penso, is my Hibernia, my Newfoundland. When in Cork do as the Daneburghers do, Momonian buggery in the Southernmost bunghole."

"This ... (between pants) is ... my Mistress ... Quickly ... my Virgin Queen."

The last vowel was a long exclamation of rediscovery.

"She has, I swear it, riven me to the quick. Late of London, now of Cork. Mistress of The Fortunate Isles."

I broke out into uncontrollable laughter. To see Raleigh totally naked save for his sea boots presiding over his mistress's rump, as if she were a man-of-war in full sail. She was wearing a henna'ed wig and white make-up that gave her face an enamelled smoothness not at all unlike our great Queen and Empress. My laughter totally undid my erection, and the two girls from the other room came in to investigate the raucousness. When they saw Raleigh in full sail they too started to laugh. By now he was waving and saluting to imaginary crowds gathered on the quays to greet his return. Alice came towards him and presented him with a bouquet of roses and cold broccoli which she gathered up from the table. This done she tweaked his declining manhood.

"*Imperator non renovator*," he chanted, staring at his flaccid member. "Let the organ into timidity shrink, so we may be at peace to recover our strength for the great trial that is to come. But Father Pensivo, have you done the deed?"

"No," I replied. "Later."

By now all desire had abated. I could not renew the seriousness necessary for the persuance of those intricate solemnities of full erotic fervour. My devotion had subsided, along with my member. The girls seemed in no way to mind. I had not asked the first one, the masterful one, what they called her. I did so.

"Mary," she replied.

Mistress Quickly was telling Raleigh of her time in London. She had known Marlowe, the poet, and Shakespeare, before he began to write. I had heard something of this last name, and as soon as I heard of him I had known I didn't like it. An image came into my mind of me walking down a street in – where was it? – Italy, Padua, maybe, or even Florence. A blue sky, solemn statuary, my muscles easy with the pleasure of being alone and confident. And then this figure, whom I knew to be Shakespeare, walking towards me, a long phallus in his hand, multicoloured like a barber's pole, with ribbons of blue and green and red flowing out of the carved glans at the tip. The phallus seemed to have some kind of elaborate system of joints and articulations, for as he waved it, it undulated up and down along its length.

I did not like the name. Shakespeare.

"But Marlowe was a sullen boy," Mistress Quickly was saying. "A horny lad, with like inclinations to yourself, Master Raleigh. Fond of the dark. 'I must probe,' he would say. 'I must probe.' He told me once that the reason he liked boys was because he wanted to be a father but could not stomach a wife. 'You women, you terrify me,' he would say, sitting close to me, tears in his eyes. 'I do not know why you scare me so. But you, my Queen,' (he also called me that; Shakespeare never would, 'twas always Mistress Quickly with him, or just plain Nan, and I never saw him cry) but anyway Marlowe would say, 'you, my Queen, you make me feel comfortable.' And that is all I want for you men, to be comfortable. A little money passes, but then this is the arrangement. Is it not better to keep your privacy orderly and allow us to take your secrecy and bury it? No dog can dig that up, even you, Master Raleigh, with your taste for poking around in funny places. But you're so quiet, Master Pensivo. Have you known Marlowe?"

"Briefly," I said. He was a victim. He wanted to be liked, as I did, but he gave himself over to authority by publicising his misdemeanours through recklessness. He wanted to be loved by those in power. He wanted a father and thought he could get one. I didn't and I knew in any case that life's early misfortunes cannot be cancelled by subsequent devotion. By the time we realise a need we are ravenous, impatient and importunate, even in sentiment. Hence Marlowe's tears. His refusals and his deliberate cultivation of danger. What she said of Shakespeare intrigued. Yes, even from the name I knew he'd not cry too easily. I was to meet him in London later, but even then I could feel that he and his work would have the cold vehemence of a loneliness that doesn't crack. Now I have seen some of his plays, and I am glad, in one sense, that while he has been enjoying his popularity in London, I have been mostly in Ireland. And glad too that he is far from me in the world of the theatre. He diversifies speech; I unify and scrutinise. All my stanzas a wariness, suspicion, until the light breaks and I am seeing again the world invigorated by the living word that I strive to maintain.

"Strife-torn Pensivo from the wilds of Cork," Raleigh said, jeering. "Weren't you fond of the Marlovian fondling? Soft-at-tease Kit, hand in placket to pluck out the moon. A bauble for yearnlings."

"Raleigh, you know I abominate that softness in him. He is the future. All remorse one minute: the rest he'd cauterise you in the arse. Dreaming of impossibility always."

"I thought you were the idealist, Spunce?"

"That may be, but his intelligence is soft, not pure. He wants ease; he wants the material world to be always still to him, so he can jack off to it."

"And you? Define yourself."

"I want to impregnate the world with the images of my mind. Vivification and unity. He, he is preparing his regret on the first sign of contact. He doesn't understand the great machine of being: he closes it down, walks away, feels tragic, and succumbs. An escapadoe."

"Cunts be praised; I don't think I've heard you talk so much for ages, not since the days of Sidney and that night of Giordano's fun-talk at Greville's."

That sad Italian face of Giordano Bruno, the Nolan, coming on the night barge, losing his way in the open sewers of London, composing his mind as he came, singing to the boatman soft Neapolitan songs of the breath of oranges, revolving in his head the image of Elizabetta, turning until the white enamelled face shot out rays of light, discs of speech that were not words but co-ordinations of the blood. Signs of being. She had the sun in her blood. A lion guarded her virgin channel. He was her unicorn. His thought spinning out to a fiery point of vision. He sang again, and we, waiting in the dark, could hear him; and I cried, and I knew Philip Sidney and Fulke Greville were crying too. We knew that Bruno had divined our England for us, its secret beauty, its sharp violence, its strength, better than any of us could ever do alone. We chilled at the thought.

"It is," I remember saying foolishly, "the descendant of Aeneas coming across the dark flood. We are England re-vivified. He comes to tell us how to build." Then silence. The boat slammed against the wharf.

V

IT WAS WHILE we were at sea between Ireland and
England that I had my dream of Raleigh, which I call
the "The Healing". My poem, in its great stack of
paper, was in a chest by my bedside. I had been leafing
through some parts of it, considering it strange,
wondering if I had ever written these stanzas – they
seemed out of time, as if I had written them without
knowing. Where had all the time gone that had been
occupied with its composition? In any case, I fell asleep,
dropping into a warm haze.

There was the movement of a scarlet cloak in the dim
hinter-world; voices speaking in Irish; then a great gaunt
face, care-troubled, woe-haunted, speechlessly proclaim-

ing as the words were silenced, a face from underwave. A nerve in my head started at what it was mouthing, and it surfaced in my dream: "Kinsale", "Kinsale". This faded, then I heard a child cry, bleating out of pure sorrow and hunger. It was in a damp hovel on an island in a lake in far County Cork. Ragged and thin, its limbs worked in a feverish grief. Beside it was its mother, dugs collapsed, every drop of milk squeezed out, her eyes closing in futile exhaustion.

"Who may forgive?" a voice said, quietly. "Who may forgive?"

A knight of arms wearing a red cross on his white tunic strode in, and, pulling the child from its mother's dry breast, smashed its head against a wall. His face was covered in iron. A white stream of breath issued from his visor with every exhalation. He grabbed the child by the legs, dangled it in front of the mother's tired eyes, who now could do nothing, not even protest, so deep her exhaustion. He unsheathed his sword and, lifting it high above his head, cut the child perfectly in half. Great red daubs of blood stained his tunic.

"My word is Justice," he breathed in a plume of white from the grille of his helmet.

"There must be no more sorrow," the mother cried. "Not after this. All my nerves are open. You can do anything to me now. Any punishment now is only what I expect."

He lifted the sword again and cut deeply into her head.

"Again."

This time the heavy blade sank into her neck, opening

right down to a point between her hanging dugs.

"It is so easy," he said. "Easy."

She sank to her knees, saying: "I am satisfied now. This is the whole pain. You have shown me all. Ransack, ransack your nerves and you will find me in there. Your tenderness that would keep you from your true ambitions. Your fiery achievement, all to be yours, in time. You are thrilled now, knowing this secret. And it will not often be so clear to you as in this our secret compliance. Your breath will convert to energy so pure as to be invisible. A crackle along the air. Your mind has ceased to hurt, for a time. I am glad of your relief. But it will convert and I'll be you and you me. And then you will know this extreme pleasure."

The knight at arms lifted up his visor. I saw the blue eyes weeping. It was Raleigh.

He left the house and headed for the sea. He galloped his horse fiercely until he reached a range of hills behind which he knew stretched the Atlantic. He slowed the horse down to a trot and slowly climbed a rough wood which passed between two dark peaks. He descended into a small cove in which the thunder of the sea was amplified hollowly. Before him a flash of gold in the dull light. A knight at arms clad in blue-grey armour, the helmet off, was sitting on a rock facing the pounding sea. The gold was a shock in this place of bleak red stone. The knight turned and Raleigh saw that the face was that of a girl, and that she had been grieving. She snatched up the helmet which lay by her side and put it on, its red plume dancing in the air.

"Why assume your battledress again? Why not be easy," Raleigh said. "I have a lance of tenderness may do fair battle with your soft quiet, may afflict it with deepening. This metal, which makes us so alike, may be laid aside to attend to a prolonged encounter, a serene delight this quiet day, where no one will come to threaten us. We can enact all manner of jovial possibilities: there need be no restraint upon us, save what we invent. The air is temperate, though stormy. A gloom to make a world in, this afternoon for love."

She had mounted her horse. She threw up her visor and said to him boldly: "Sir, either you leave me in peace immediately, or you will have my lance in your guts."

Raleigh laughed. She rushed at him and he had scarcely time to lift his lance before hers had slammed into his stomach. Her impetus carried him off his horse and he fell against a large rock. The lance broke through the mail below his chest and sank right in, fracturing his spine, which snapped in half. He fell sideways onto the broken half of the lance still stuck in him, ripping open the wound in his belly and shifting the entire spinal column a number of inches.

She dismounted then, taking off her helmet again, kneeled down and drank from the blood which poured from his open stomach. Her yellow locks were stained when she raised her bloody face. Not smiling, speechless, she mounted up again and rode away.

There was silence. Raleigh could hear his groans echoing in the sea chamber all around the cliffs. His vision blurred. And he went over into the sleep before death.

The sea quietened into complete stillness. The sun brightened and the surface of the water assumed a deep turquoise. The waves subsided into slight stirrings of white turning over on the shore. An underwater music sounded, a strange blaring, intermixed with the thin plaint of flutes and a rustling softness of strings. A smiling head broke surface about ten yards out. It had two horns and yellow hair. Around the head the blue water bubbled and one after another more heads came through. The creatures swam towards the shore and came out of the sea towards the body, singing. Their bodies were of green scale that caught the sunlight. They carried him between them into the sea. Again there was quiet. The horse stood. Occasionally a muscle twitched along her flesh and set her trappings jingling. There was another burst of music, mingled voices and instruments, and then, again, silence.

The cove relaxed into the sunlight which already had begun to dry the knight's red blood.

As he went under the waves his hair was borne upwards in a slow undulation. The weight of the armour meant that he sank swiftly. The creatures guided him in under a rock, through a crevice which opened into a large undersea room that had a green air of its own. Blue torches made the light tremble between two colours. The creatures carried the body to a pallet of sea-moss and laid him there. Then they divested him of his armour. His face, softer now in death, was white and serene, the eyes closed. They removed the breastplate, then the mail, then the body leather, and there, on Raleigh's chest, were two female breasts. The male hair of the breastbone had shrivelled to a cobwebby dryness, and one of the creatures brushed it off to reveal the new shapeliness of the full breasts. When the lower part of the armour was removed it was evident that the male genitals had also gone, in their place the perfection of a dark mound of Venus, within, twin coral lips.

Soundlessly the creatures left him in the undersea cave, the green light moving on the still features, stricken but at peace.

Some time later the creatures came back through the crevice leading out to the sea-floor. They gabbled and talked and gesticulated. When one came forward and took Raleigh's head in his arms and stroked it with two webbed fingers there was a start of life in the eyes. Then nothing.

"She is still far away from us," the creature said. "She has to be won back not through what we can do, but from the efficacy of someone else's love coming through to us here. The man who put him here must free him. And," (turning around, facing out of the dream, looking me straight in the face, the green skin smooth with certainty, the eyes bright with accusation and hope) "that is you, Spenser, that is you. You have put her here. You must now judge yourself and see how good your life is. Most of your talk of love's a distraction, a confection on top of your anxiety to hate. What of those little thrills of pleasure at any little bit of sad news? I do not say this to compound your self-hate. There is much worse to come and you will have played your part. But the shame is not yours or anyone's specifically: it lies on you all, you humans, with your passion for alertness, extinction, and imprisonment.

And the worst kind of imprisonment is that which you inflict on her, the one behind me. When will you perform the healing?"

I was awakened out of my dream, the talk of the green man still resounding in my mind. His voice was deep and slow, and it seemed as if the crash of the waves on the timbers of the ship carried with them his words, but they were becoming inchoate as I came out of my dream. I could see the grey pages of my manuscript in the chest at the side of my bed. All that effort; all that discrimination; all that manipulation in stanza and image and line and picture; all that learning; but none of it certain. Why could I not embark into certainty? Why could I not allay all my vagueness. My work was a colonisation of incoherence by meanings, but they all added up to foolishness, a stupid knight fucking in the plain. Nowhere, nothing, no light. The labour; the endless futile scrawl of it.

That girl in the cave. So hard to keep her picture in my mind. Already she was disappearing back into a blur. Poor Raleigh.

VI

LONDON IN SUNLIGHT. We had arrived. The tall buildings were touched by the soft air as we sailed up the Thames. A smell of richness and power came down-river, a spiciness mingled with the usual smell of shit. Bright colours caught the eye: men and women stopped what they were doing on the banks to look at the ship coming up the river. A child's face looked out of a tiny attic window: he put out a hand with difficulty and waved. The gutterings on the buildings looked secure and well-maintained; the drainpipes fixed to the walls seemed firm. As we moved upstream the sun caught the small panes of windows, so that flashes of light moved with us. A dog ran along the bank, barking. He would stop, bark, then run on again. I looked sideways at Raleigh: he was smiling with pleasure and breathing those rich smells. "She is still here," he said, "still here. The Old Whore."

A grave figure in black with a funny yellow hat turned into a milliner's shop; a red-faced woman with sleeves rolled up stopped to look at us. She put both hands on her hips and stood with feet wide apart, the dirty white calico of her clothing emphasising her chapped arms. She watched us, her head slowly turning as we moved. A roar of laughter came from an inn, and a drunk staggered out, shouting. I felt puzzled and excited by the big strangeness of the city I knew so well. Streams of sewage flowed in from minor tributaries. We passed an open market where the brightly coloured awnings caught the eye. Oranges, apples, pineapples were on display. A mountebank with a huge brown floppy hat screamed in derision at his audience. London.

VII

THE UNEASE OF those first days in London I shall never forget. Raleigh disappeared, whoring maybe, or to see some of his strange friends, those given to alchemical studies. He had told me something of a glass he wished to make, that would, through concentration, open up the vista of the place you wanted to see. It was a glass that would enable the possessor to view backwards and forwards in time, and which would enable him to see strange lands and ways. Raleigh had this idea, which he would speak of incessantly when drunk, of a golden world in the Americas, a city with most elaborate spires designed to capture all the effulgence of the sun's rays and transmit them to certain rooms, known as *stanzi d'or*, in which anything introduced would convert to pure gold on the instant. I suspected he was amongst the Jews in the lower parts of the city, drinking, and discussing the grinding of lenses.

For my own part I would lie in a vacant state these days, trying to compose laudatory verses about London and the virtue of the Queen's presence, but she seemed much more absent from me there than she had done in Ireland. At Kilcolman writing *The Faerie Queene* on those calm nights when she walked in the room, she smiled and was kind, subduing all the violence my mind would seethe with into harmony; but in London there was nothing but a sad sterility.

My landlord was a dwarf from Algiers. One evening I had been drinking wine too copiously at the tavern and when I came back the dwarf, who had taken the name Astolfo – his house was known as "Astolfo's Garden" – was sitting over the fire, the two tiny feet resting on the bar of the grate.

"Ah, Sir," said he, "you should return to Ireland. And I should go back to Africa."

"Why?" I asked.

"We have no Queen, you and I. The future will be for such as us, but in our time now we are unhappy."

"But I am devoted to the Queen. This is traitorous talk."

"Devotion. Absurd. That is the end. You are convincing yourself. And she will know it straight away. Their time, that of kings and queens, is going in any case and they know that. This gardening, building, ceremony –

useless. They are in their last hours. And they force you and those like you to worship them. To praise them as if they were God himself. They seem to you to be composed of a different element. You think of them as having fire for blood. But no, they shit, do they not? But you know that only too well, you celebrators; your minds are always on shit."

"How do you know so much about my mind, dwarf?"

"I know of your poetry and versings. Every half-wit afficionado in the streets rehearses your name. But I know you from here" (pointing to his stomach). "I know your little compliances and surrenders, your little powers of wheedling, and I have decided to speak out to you and tell you my story of the interior."

"What story is that?"

"Well, before I left Algiers to come north, knowing that a fortune could be made in these climes, I went on a trip south to Yorubaland, near the line, to consult with the priestess of the Osun river. Her prophetic and healing powers are renowned throughout our continent. She can speak all the African languages, and she can kill by a mere look. I went to get advice. I wanted to know if my trip north to the cold land of Elizabeth the white queen would be prosperous. It took me five weeks to reach the sacred river of Osun. The river speaks, so they say, speaks to all of Africa, and to the rest of the world, too, but they say in Africa that the world no longer can hear. The Osun's water, a trace of it, is in the glass of wine which I propose we take now, in memory of the goddess. Her waters are everywhere, even in this flesh" (plucking at his fat jowl).

He went to a dark cabinet and filled out two glasses of wine. Lifting his, he said: "From Algiers to the goddess. The priestess hears the water and tells you what it says to you. What it is saying to you."

"What was she like?"

"She was by the waterside, attended by her husbands, of which she has thirteen. The requirement is that she listen and watch all movement along the river-bank. The flight of a bird upstream, a yellow streak in the arduous light; the sound of a bullfrog yapping; the drone of the beetles at midday; even the way the leaves shift their dusty surfaces to the intense heat – all these have to be noticed. When she is fully attentive her eyes darken and all she sees is the river, and it is a movement of dark light, a coursing through the air, and it flows *through* her head and out again, the entire body of the river, and she knows all things to come."

"Did she tell you of England?"

"She spoke of the beauty of the north, of a radiance breaking out of a northern river, brother to the Osun, called Thames. She told how the river built a city of glass and colour, and that he walked in a white face and elaborate jewellery, that he took a female body called Elizabeth. He wished many men to share that body of Elizabeth, but there was never to be any. She was to be lonely. She was the last manifestation of the river. After that rivers would no longer walk in men or women in that country. The country would prosper but never again would it have the friendship of its rivers and they would remain strange.

"She told me I should go, that that country was a place for men to thrive, fearful men, like me and you. The fearless men would never again be esteemed. There was one in particular, she said, and she stopped for a while to listen. Tears filled her eyes and she buried her face in her hands. She said that his name was 'Water', that of all his sons Thames loved him most of all, but that he should finish his days under a great white sea, locked in another man's ill will and fear. That man could heal him, if he so desired, and in healing him he would heal himself, but that that fate was not certain. There was to be no general healing again in that country; its love was to be private and anxious; its citizens over-fed, mostly incapable of listening."

I was appalled by the dwarf's revelation. He had divined something of my dream about Raleigh. It was clear that my business was unfinished. And the Queen's nickname for Raleigh was always "Water". She would talk of him as her watery poet, her fair expanse, Father Ocean, safeguard of the realm. But what was the relation between Raleigh and me, and why did my dream convert him into a girl in the undercave?

"So," the dwarf continued, "the priestess took me back to her house, and brought me into her secret room. In a large cage hanging from the ceiling was a creature that looked half-man, half-ape. He spoke to her in a strange language and she answered back. She told me he was her son, fathered on her by the river Osun."

"But you said the Osun was female?" I said.

"Yes, I asked her that too. She looked at me and

41

laughed. "How little you northerners know. Osun is female, but to mate with me, which she does every moon, she enters a creature of the forest and sends him to me at the night of the full moon. When she stops coming like this then I know another priestess is to be chosen and my work is done. When it is done I shall be glad, for then I will become the goddess and it will be my turn to become male each night of the full moon."

"So, dwarf, was that all she told you? Was there no more about England. I am not interested in these savage rites, even worse than the Romish abominations of the country I am forced to live in."

"She went on endlessly about England and poets and women. I cannot recall. She foretold that there would be a man who would have a brain of ice and whose hatred of all womankind would be so intense that he would put many of the sisterhood to death. But there was no escape; it was all written. The country would go more into the head. I remember her pointing at her black matted skull, her eyes wide open in terror as she recounted this. The country, she said, would organise itself so that all the limbs would become weary, being physically encumbered by an expansion of thought and administration. Men would build stone columns and windows and great houses to allay the emptiness of the head, but there was to be no such ease. She said there was a country, a cold place out in the Western Seas, whose fate was totally bound up with that land of Elizabeth. That land was the land where England's justice would be tested, and found wanting. She knew this because the Osun spoke at length with the

Shannon on these matters, two great sister-rivers feeding into the Atlantic. England, she said, would send all her bad men there, and only one would really triumph, the man with the brain of ice.

"This, then, Master Spenser, is my voyage to the interior. It took me five more weeks to return to Algiers. And then no great time elapsed before I came here, following my fortune. But you, you are not a fortunate man, even less fortunate than I."

"That is so. Why Astolfo? Do you know?"

"You want completeness. You would like your words to be part of a commonweal, so you're always after authority, hoping those in authority will favour you. But they hate you. You are poison, *poison* to them."

"Why?"

"Why? Because they realise you want nothing less than that their blood should speak; that their eyes should conform precisely to their words – *your* words, if you could manage it. You are a dangerous man, in love with totality, and they are right to distrust you. Your time will come. But it will be a cruelty impossible even to envisage now. And the poor faulty statesmen know this and try to hold you back from eminence well aware of the damage you do to them inside. You and your total speech. Speech at the cost of what?"

At this the picture of Raleigh as a girl came into my mind. The girl in the green cave, not breathing, locked into the adamantine rock, waiting for me, my sympathy, to open her up.

VIII

THE FOLLOWING IS a scrap which I found among my papers relating to estates at Kanturk. I enclose it here. I do not fully understand it. Nor do I remember writing it, but it seems to bear on the dwarf's consultations with the African river.

Two men in a rocky place, one complaining of his shoes, the other philosophical.

"What are we doing here, Didi?"

"Don't know, Gogo. We are waiting for sympathy. It's easy for them out there in that world of clean lavatories and shower taps. But they keep us here."

"And all the time we grow female."

"So we do, Didi."
"Doo didi doo. Nipples on us two."

Colin Clout.

IX

LIGHT WAS SINKING. The sun was shining through the blue glass of the chamber, dully illuminating the cloth of gold on the brocaded chairs. The Queen sat, breathing the blue-gold air, watchful of the effect her presence had.

Raleigh and I had come through the sea of the court. It was an orchestration pulled and tightened, relaxed and eased, by the tiniest movements of the Queen. Her presence, an electric gloom, a gold radiance, dominated everything, even the slightest of bodily twitches. Even when they were not looking directly at her, all her courtiers took in every movement she made, each indication of the head, the brilliant flash of her sable eyes.

A thrill of physical self-disgust and hate ran through the room if she spoke to anyone: and the person honoured so would glow briefly, strut, all power, for five minutes. The object of incalculable waves of envy and hate. And then, that brief intensity gone, he would lapse into the fright of expectancy in which he would share with the rest of the moving unity of tension, crossing and tangling in the lines of negotiation centred on her. And then he, too, would hate the next one to whom she would incline her head or grace with a look.

I thought I got the old smell that I always got at court, a faint, distant, remote, but insistent aroma of shit. The medium through which all their refined emotions of envy and hatred ran was composed of the very finest distillation of excrement, urine and sweat. A detritus of loving and agony and self-hate. All looking for love, for notice, for significance. And I too, loving that faint smell of English shit, that dimly apprehended golden effulgence rendered divine by power and money and tension. This was civilization.

Raleigh, who knew how to play this elaborate dance, and who had written a poem in celebration of its finesse, worked his way from the periphery into the centre of her attention. From the edge I watched her incline her head to his laughing mouth, and watched the strained face break into a wintry smile. When her lips opened fully I saw two rotten teeth.

They started to walk around the room and the courtiers began, imperceptibly, to shift with their movement, all kinds of fine adjustments taking place. A youthfulness began to manifest itself in the Queen's bearing; her step lightened and she began to talk to Raleigh with animation. He was cajoling her: they had found a vein of mutual self-mockery where they were at rest, both speaking frankly to each other. The mood lightened in the room and others now began to walk about and converse, talking animatedly to one another, in sad mimicry of the central relaxation.

At one point Raleigh looked at me, a surprising flash of blue, even as he was in mid-sentence with the Queen, as if to say, "I've got her." Then, later, another look, towards the door of the ante-chamber, guiding me towards it. I moved through the network of negotiation and got to the door, panelled in blue and white, embossed with cupidons, just after they did. She proceeded through, giving both of us a flirtatious sign to follow. I looked behind just before I went through and saw a sea of faces, all turned towards us, looking at us in a silence of baffled hate. I knew there were at least a half a dozen who would kill me at that moment.

Raleigh had arranged this meeting so I could recite to the Queen parts of my poem. I felt ludicrous, a half-monkey in a cage, but hopeful too, thinking that the authority she represented would be touched by my images of order, glory and strength.

"Does our Irish lad need a harp to accompany himself with?" she asked.

"No," I replied foolishly. "Madam, your court would not be the place for such Hibernian fooleries."

"Tyrone is a gentleman. He is entitled to our best regards. I like a man who has the courage to be himself."

"Madam, Tyrone is a most untrustworthy knave. When he drinks at night his toast is: 'Would this wine were the blood of the Queen of England'."

What was I doing? I was toadying and talking too much and arguing with her as well. I knew what she would say next. Whenever I wanted to appeal to authority by reassuring it of my goodwill it immediately shifted its ground, and I was left a nincompoop. Same as now. I knew it was going to come.

"That is a fine manly toast. I'd prefer that than that a hundred miserable yellow-brained stinking cajolers should drink the health of their loving Queen. Hoping all the time for a miserable knighthood, so they can lord it over their neighbours. Oh these soft-brained English, not like my Raleigh – a Celt, deep from the valley at the edge of this soft-bellied country. For a poet you have a remarkably innocent grasp of affairs, Master Spenser."

Raleigh smiled.

"You are being hard on my friend, Madam. He has been rusticated in Ireland too long: his conversation there is with servants and underlings; he needs the sharp stimulation of office, of London. He is loyal, Madam, devoted to your good self, as I am. Be kind to those who love you truly. His poem is one long love tribute to you, which will enable you to live forever in men's eyes and minds."

"Water, how many times have promises of this kind been made to me? Every poet thinks he has the secret of the bestowal of immortality. And they are all weak-kneed infiltrators, each manjack, that is if they are any good. The bad ones, they are the idealists, and are fit for nothing, not even to be stewards of the Royal toilet."

It was quite plain I had little chance of advancement from this source. I was speechless. Now was the moment to be bold and speak through this restraint she was imposing on me, to open her up, face her. I could see Raleigh waiting for me to move in. All I could manage was self-humiliation, to begin with, but as I spoke my confidence grew, nervously.

"Madam, I am sorry that I have wasted your time and that of my good friend, Sir Walter. I shall by your good leave retire to Ireland and there live in obscurity. There is little I can think of to say to you that would impress. Now is the time for me to embark upon an apology: if I were to try to insinuate myself with you now I know I could never again be the man I would wish to become for your sake. If I could manufacture now speech for my future comfort and safety it would be untrue. And you know that. And why do you expect it of me?"

"Ah, so the quiet one speaks after all, Water. I" (to me) "expect nothing from you. But it is a sign of a man's intelligence that he does not remain altogether silenced by authority. But your reply is trouble to me. Explain."

"I cannot. I have not been gifted with a ready tongue to cancel offence and conceal it with good humour. Nor am I good at passionate self-justification which works only to flatter the other's authority."

"You are a Puritan, Master Spenser. You are cold. You wish not to belong with the life of men. In fact you see us as monkeys, do you not?"

How did she see that I still had in the back of my mind,

50

somewhere, the picture of Astolfo's half-man half-ape? How could she see so far into me? I looked at those sable eyes again, the whites brightened with nightshade, and I was stung by a sense of her majesty. She was fire, the fire of her father's syphilis and the fire of the sun itself. I felt parched and dry. A lizard on a great sea of dry sand, feverishly pumping its body up and down, waiting. I was subdued. She knew it.

"So, Master Spenser, you must forgive an old lady's vagaries. Take no notice. I know some of your poems, such sweet carolling of the year's phases. Please, recite me some of your verse, my Irish English bard."

So I did. I recited stanzas from the story of the British maid, and as I did so I had the sense, moving in my verses, that she and I, who belonged together, shared a peace in the rhymes and balancings, with agonies averted, chaos controlled. She was the spirit that moved in my language; I knew it now for definite, standing awkwardly before her, telling of the love that brought us together. Her eyes were closed, and I knew, somewhere, she was crying at what she was hearing. Not now, but as a girl again, looking out through a leaded window, watching a man ride away slowly without turning back. The girl was crying now between us and she knew I understood her quiet, a quiet so great it would consume all England. And I, from Ireland, telling her this, from Irene's shore my tale of her youth, her loss, her quiet. What I was saying in these verses, now I knew, was the final interminable parting between her and me. The verses were the prologed valediction, sustained through sheer energy of will, and attentiveness, to our forever severed unity. In the breaking it would be my skill that would dominate, and that she knew too: that was part of her grief. I had subdued her.

"That was beautiful, Master Spenser. Come tomorrow. I am tired now. Come alone. I wish to speak to you. Come at three in the afternoon. Goodbye, Water."

We took our leave through the room of state where the courtiers seemed fuddled, lacklustre, sedulously ignoring the envied two who had been closeted with the Queen.

The air was mild and pure after the stifled atmosphere at court. A grey sky loomed. A barge sailed slowly upriver. A rat plopped into the water, teeth bared as it swam furiously, an erratic glide just under the water's surface.

"You've done it, Spunse," he said, "you've got the private audience. Perhaps now we can rig out an expedition together and get you out of this turmoil of versing. Not good for you. All that silence."

"I have little expectation of anything from her. I think she dislikes me."

"Why? She's always sharp and challenging. Always difficult."

"No, it isn't just that. She hates my being. She knows too much about my interior. What I am like inside. She knows I am a jungle. And that ... well...."

"Spenser," Raleigh said, looking at me uneasily, "I think Ireland has really begun to affect you. You're going native. All this talk of the interior and the underworld. Leave that to the Irish druidic enthusiasts. Your virtue is your clarity, man, your virility. Less of this unknown inner-life stuff. We live in glittering surfaces. The underneath? Who can know it? It is the riches of this world for which we have to strive."

Even as he was saying this I knew he was opting for something rather than believing it. It was a prejudice. I had his measure now.

"You hope and pray that that is so, Raleigh, do you not? You think of your life as a voyage conducted along bright even surfaces, drawn by attraction to that which is most desirable. But that is innocence, and you are no innocent. And you are not going to tell me you live in this unknowing?"

"Look, Spunse. There is wealth. I want it. And by Christ I'm going to have it. And I will take any means to acquire it."

"But then you must know that you are putting yourself in fief to a hopelessly simple world that will, as sure as that turd lies on the ground ahead of us, trick you."

"If, as you say, the Queen mistrusts you, she may be right to doubt a mind capable of thinking like this. It is outrageous, Spenser. What trickery are you at? You *are* a jungle, damn you."

"But Raleigh, my friend, yours is not a mind that craves reassurance. I know this. Why opt for the self-congratulating practicality of the worldly-wise, their pathetic deceptions and collusions? Your mind is venturous."

As I said this, the presumption of it struck me. Who was I, an upstart worldling, to be talking like a preacher to a man of Raleigh's solid depth. My ideas seemed thin. But somehow he didn't know his strength, and not knowing it meant he had a weakness that could be, had been, exploited.

Even as we talked I knew I was damaging him, opening up to him a version of himself, inside, that would work like a poison in his veins, paralysing the solid man into inertia and quiet. He was like a lover whom one likes to damage in the name of kindness, understanding and sympathy. The love that is cruelty, the love that is violence, the promised heaven, the floor of which is hell riddled with fiery bars of anxiety and hopelessness. "Be bold," I heard myself saying to myself. "Be bold. Be not too bold."

I looked at my friend's open face, stilled and pale with unusual bafflement.

X

A T THREE THE next day I went to court, alone. Arriving at the room of state, an usher, knowing immediately who I was, conducted me to a separate apartment to wait for the Queen. The room was all blue brocade, heavy curtains of dark Prussian velvet made a theatre of the cloudy sky. It was filled with a steady even light. In one corner a white bust of a Caesar shone, cooly. On the wall facing the window was a canvas depicting a classical scene. A youth with pale gold skin played a set of flat pipes. Above his head the vines bore clusters of dark fruit. In the distance a city shimmered. Near him, on the grass, lay Venus, her eyes lidded, her soft body carelessly draped, face turned towards the spectator, away from the city's spires.

The Queen came in. A bustle of dark energy. Her hair, redder than yesterday, smote the shady light of the room. Her dress, of black heavy stuff, crackled, all menace and impatience. Her white smooth face was impassive, caked with white powder. Her eyes stared directly at me, never moving from their object of concentrated attention, which I thought of as a point somewhere behind my head. I felt foolish.

"Your life in Ireland, Master Spenser. It is pleasant, I hope. Your services are much appreciated by us. Remain assured of our good will and esteem."

This formality: I should not have expected anything else, but it was a shock, nevertheless.

"Indeed, Madam, I am honoured to be your servant."

"Remember that we always have had a most sincere regard for our loyal subjects in that unfortunate country. Those Englishmen, such as yourself, who choose to make your home there are performing a most valuable service for the crown, and for the peace which we would always bring with us."

I felt tempted to say that it was not through choice that I was living there, but sheer blind necessity, if I wasn't to be a futile scrounger in a minor office. Ireland's wastes gave me some independence and free time. That was all.

"Your Majesty may be assured of all that is in my power to ... You may be content that your rule ..."

Faltering. A quick look from those eyes that struck my nerves like a blow. A vacuum in my stomach, a void created by panic. My temples beat with fear and self-

56

disgust. I hated the bitch, and, what was worse, she knew it. At that instant I was a chieftain from some watery valley in Tyrone, stinking of cowshit, speaking Gaelic through the long drooping dark moustache, head ablaze with rancour and pride, thinking only of how I could smash that dyed head with one strong blow. And she knew it, but not a tremor of fear passed over that impassively cold, smiling face. She was used to danger and violence, used to it daily. For me it was a festivity of the nerves. And my panic, I realised with horror, was an entertainment for her. A minor afternoon diversion. I would go and be forgotten. But why was I here?

On cue to my wondering she said: "I suppose you wish to know what has brought us to ask you here?"

"Yes, indeed, Madam, I did think what small service I might be able to perform for you."

Again, Christ, I sounded like a ham. A stud, picked up in a stew for a woman's pleasure, being inspected, intimately, for the rosy blooms of syphilis, before being allowed into the lady's chamber. One of my great faults must be the talent for being humiliated.

"Your pride, Master Spenser, sorts ill with your professions of loyalty and service. But it is something of a rebellious and intractable nature we require for that with which we now crave your assistance. They are delicate matters, friend Edmund. Delicate indeed, and a severe trouble to our peace. Our magus, Dee, is, to put it mildly, an idiot, and to put matters such as I wish to discuss before him is like consulting an ape. An ape would be better, because an ape is not a bore, chattering obtusely in ludicrous rodomontade. Dee's speech is like the action of the water-closet; it washes away into dark obscurity that which is of no account in any case. You like my bold figure?"

She was flirting with me. Flirting with me about Dee's shit! I could hardly believe it. How do you respond to an invitation like this?

"Indeed, Madam, I have heard it said that his inter-pretations and advice are themselves often difficult to understand."

Soberjaws.

"But I am eager to know in what way I may be of service. I am honoured by these attentions."

The light was darkening. The figures in the painting opposite the window grew less distinct. A bell tolled slowly signalling the half-hour. I had a sense of the laboriousness of life, of its being consumed in effort and fatigue, administration, the whole attempt being to main-tain this woman and her kind in their bleak discontent, ravaging each other in their unhappiness. The energy that sustains order is derived from the impulse to destroy. Statecraft is balance. I knew that as well as anyone else, my own craft being of the same kind as that of politics. But the time comes when the attention wanders, the alertness slips, and all is embroiled in uncertainty for a time, until again a mastery of the instability appears, only to grow bleak and unhappy in its turn. I thought with a shudder of the great gong Raleigh had shown me in Youghal, its harsh metallic clang reverberating in the heavy southern air of the harbour town on a Sunday afternoon. "Beat that gong, Spunse," he had said. "Beat it and listen to the music of the spheres. It is our violence that sets the metal singing. The mysteries of the East! Nonsense. It is we out here in the West that are the mysterious ones. To ourselves. To ourselves."

Again he struck the gong and it swayed madly on its cords, harshly, noisily, until it settled down again into stillness, the notes vanishing in the air, unevenly.

"Water may have told you something of our difficulty."

"Indeed no, Madam, Sir Walter is very discreet."

"I am glad to hear it. I have been troubled with certain dreams for some months now. My dear Water tells me that you are good at deciphering signs – a hermaneut he calls you, a hermaneut in Irish trews – and has suggested that we consult you, outlining our dreams clearly. I now drop the royal we, Spenser: I need your help. These dreams afflict me most terribly. I crave interpretation. An uneasy Queen generates unease."

"If I may help, Madam."

"Well, a fortnight since it began. I dream that I am a man in armour. I come to a seashore and see a woman, who is dressed as a man, crying by the edge of the sea, speaking her grief to the waves."

My mind raced. I knew what she was going to tell me. I knew it.

"There is a storm and the wind has blown her golden hair into disarray. I am filled with lust. A huge erection makes sitting on my horse uncomfortable. I dismount and approach her. Why not? I am thinking: Why not? What does it matter who fucks whom. I am male; she is female; what need of better elaboration? I approach her

59

suggesting that we fuck, but she erupts into rage and asks me to leave. I laugh, but she mounts up. Though my erection refuses to subside I also mount up and engage with her, half playfully. She gallops at me and with a single stroke I am unhorsed, the lance all the way through my belly and out the back. I cannot believe her ferocity.

"The next bit is very strange. I am dead, I think. The storm abates, the sun shines, the sea is still, a what, a blue, a turquoise maybe? Then a green head breaks surface some small distance out. Others also break surface and the creatures swim towards me. All the time there is music. I am taken down by them, to undersea, to a cavern which is lit by blue torches. The air down there is green. They divest me of my armour but now I am female again. The leader of these creatures tells me that I am to remain thus until I am healed. I recognise my body as it was, Spenser, when I was sixteen. White and frail in the shimmering green light."

By now the room was almost entirely dark. I could just see the Queen's face, which seemed curiously relaxed. Towards the end of what she was saying her face had been turned towards the window.

Now she turned to look at me: "What does it mean, Master Spenser? I know it is of some importance, because the dream keeps on coming back, night after night, and all the images are a trouble to my thoughts. I know enough about you to know that you are expert in dealing with images and their meanings, to know that also you are concerned about us, this country, its inner state. I know this dream is to do with that, but how or why I cannot

60

guess. Can it be guessed? Can you tell me what to do?"

I could not reveal that I had had the same dream, nor that the face of one of the creatures had turned towards me to lay upon me the responsibility of releasing the girl held underwater. I had no idea what was going on, what to say, or what to do.

"I think, Madam, I can be but of scant assistance to you on this matter."

A sharp glow of contempt in the dark room. And of something else: mistrust, perhaps fear.

"It seems to me that your dream is nothing to worry about. Your girlhood is oppressed by offices of state. Your femaleness (if I may make so bold) has not been allowed to establish itself. You have had, of necessity, to be male-like to survive the rigour of office. The golden-haired girl, Madam, is you, as is the bold male knight, who would ravage the gentleness of she who grieves by the seashore. But that sheness cannot be oppressed, and defies the maleness that would seek to keep it under. And that maleness itself must become other in death, as it in itself is only partial. So the girl in the cave is you also, kept under by the sterility of the imperial legislation of maledom. You see?"

My stomach was a ball of tension. I had revealed too much and not enough. I had told her something of the personal side of the story, and in talking to her I had opened up the material for myself as well. But I had not, nor could I, tell her that I had had the same dream, that it was somehow linked with my poem, and that there was a public element in the dream, going beyond our private lives and their difficulties. And on no account could I tell her of Raleigh's presence in what was revealed to me. It was a tangle. Small beads of perspiration began to prickle on my forehead and under my arms. I had to break this spell of embarrassment.

"What you have dreamed may be connected to the future in some way I cannot decipher."

"I know," she said. "It is. Please think further on these matters, Spenser. All your former interpretation, if so it can be called, is amateurish, fabricated, literal, heavy-footed. While there is some clarity in it, I nevertheless could have worked out much of it myself. It is the latter possibility, of the future, that demands most rigorous scrutiny. And you say you cannot decipher. Try."

"I cannot, Madam. The world changes so quickly; I do not know. There is something forlorn ahead, that I know. A beast to annihilate distinction between men and women. A new age of Hermaphroditus, where love will be solely kind to kind. No opposition, a failure of the network of passages between men and women, out of which the fabric of society itself is galvanised. A killing time when mastery will be with those who most can convert their thoughts into a form of agitation that moves imperceptibly in the air, a fine effort in silence that interferes with the process of thought in others."

"I see a man," she said, "standing in the whitewashed doorway of one of the small hovels of a windswept island off the western coast of the country in which you have your residence, Hibernia. He is dressed in black shabby clothes, his arms by his sides, as he stares out into the rainy light. Under a black hat the blue eyes are looking straight into the future and he is transfixed, frozen by fear. He sees the whole terror unfold out there in the sea-light. I do not know where I get this image from, but he is there, suddenly, in my mind."

She paused. I could find nothing to say. The man she described, I could see him too, his hands by his sides, two large patches on his trousers where the knees had come through.

"It is curiously relaxing to have you to speak to thus, Master Spenser. It is as if the movement of my mind clarifies for me as I talk to you, though I do not understand that which arises into my thought. But the difficulty is opened, there is a relief. Life is so tight. It is hard to speak freely. And you realise, of course, that even this mild intimacy that I am now allowing myself with you will mean that you will never be allowed permanently to return from Ireland. To be my confidant, which you are now becoming, means that you must stay in Hibernation."

"Madam," I said (thinking as quickly as I could, striving against anxiety and futility), "Madam, I do not think I wish any longer to return to England. I love her too dearly to live here all the time. When I think in Kilcolman of the streets of your capital, I often break down and weep, overcome with loss and hopeless love, but I am no longer for these shores, this serenely lovely land of sharp mornings and deep summery valleys. I know now that I must make my England in my head, to glorify her forever."

Why can I not have more guile? Why do I reveal

everything so easily? What misfortune made me want to explain myself? She had little grasp of what I was trying to say. I had once again talked myself into a too complex silence, one that made us both even more uncomfortable than we had been already. How I longed to be out of that stuffy room, the ever-growing interior darkness, the faint glimmering of light from the windows, the over-ornate furniture.

Again, going too far, recklessly, unaccountably, coming in: "I think our England" (all the time thinking that it was *her* England I was talking about) "is passing. You do a holding action, you maintain balance, but these fine checks must eventually fail. We" (meaning *you*) "are already dead, and we feel the accusation in the eyes of those still living, those to whom the future will belong. They are concocting in their heads already little patterns, geometrical figures, formulae, ways of ordering their gardens" (might as well put Bacon in the shit if I could, that louse) "that have for their object our annihilation. In quiet they develop the little mental signals to exclude us, words that they say quietly to themselves at night to console them in their tribulation, which they are sure will soon cease. They have theorems about surds and conic sections, and about the cycloid, that will rule us out. They are killing us with their thinking, and they know it, even though they want to pretend that it is all learning. Learning? It is loutishness."

A small, tired, grey, kindly face, looking, eyes blinking back tears. A severe face, hair cropped, glasses glinting.

Why do I care so much? He is one that also is to survive all the ravages. And I, too, a soul for survival. The kindly ferret-face refusing to eat the shit like the rest. And I, shit-eater, talking myself into false positions, emotional no-gos, away from all that would affiance me with this room, this woman. My own good fortune. All speech is as nothing, or so I felt as I was struggling with my language that afternoon, when I had revealed I was not sure what, but whatever it was, it was too much. She knew now for certain that I was a dangerous man, because I had some grasp of the fine lineations of hatred, anger and fear as they threaded through the web of invisible fire that she occupied in her breathing. She knew that I understood how she was threatened by the imminent collapse of that inner tightness that sustained her crackling assurance, her bustling energy. And my knowing was an affront. But I also had a pretty good idea that she would want me back again, for I didn't know what humiliation, but want me back she would. And I, of course, would assent, always the ready Guy, the Irish courtier most eager to comply.

"It would seem, Spenser, that you have given most cautious consideration to many of the things with which we find ourselves occupied."

The royal "we" again. The interview, the intimacy, the danger was drawing to a close. I actually began to feel a little lonely. A hankering for the sensual excitement, the electric sense of danger that was there some moments ago, took hold of me.

She had put a spell on me, through giving me to

understand that she had fathomed me out in my innermost lurkings.

Christ, she was Jesuitical. She had got in there. *She* had fucked *me*. And I was looking for the intimacy again, already, as she, formally, easily, elegantly, was drawing the afternoon, now almost completely dark, to a close. I wanted the closeness (so briefly established, so grounded in estrangement and embarrassment, so difficult to know precisely who was hoodwinking whom) to continue into the strengthening dark of evening. How attracted to the court I was after all, and I having just made my little speech about not really belonging in England through the intensity of my love for her. I, a gabbler, talking myself out of what I most desire, to talk myself into an estrangement from that to which I most belong. I, a foosterer, at a loss for words, mastered (mistressed?) by the lady so severely drawing our interview to a close. But she would want me back, for sure, this Irish tramp all at sea in London, his one true place.

"I would request you, if you can find time from the pressing business of having your book set by the printers, to come and speak with me again. There is another matter I would discuss with you."

"More dreams, Madam?"

"Yes, Master Spenser, more dreams, to which I would direct your attention. Private things through which I detect matters of greater moment. Your interpretation of today is riddling and uncertain, my Erse hermaneut. Indeed I did think, at times, that you were unravelling your own mystery. Which is far from mine."

Distances, cold distances.

"Goodbye, Madam."

"Goodbye, Master Spenser."

XI

"WORDS, WORDS, WORDS."
Shakespeare was drunk. Raleigh had been telling me that when in his cups he said very little. That his favourite phrase was the one he had come out with now. He was rolling his head around on his dirty white ruff. Balding, his skin was bad; his eyes, when open, bleary. His face was grizzled, not having been barbered for a few days. He was singing softly to himself. Some nonsensical rhyme. This. This was to be England's Apollo!

His head collapsed onto his shoulder and he left it there. A red eye opened, looking fixedly at me. For a moment I was fearful that I was in for the usual drunken writer's argument, all antagonism to begin with, then the usual patching up and the false fellowship, and the poisonous good nature. I hate writers, most of all poets. No, this was different. There was a warmth in the air around us. It actually began to feel warmer. A faint, very faint, so attenuated as to be almost ghostly, scent of flowers hung in the air for a moment, then was gone. But it left an impression. A sunburnt face came into my mind, laughing, turning to look at me from its occupation. Peace and silence. The quiet earth forever waiting for us to give it speech, and we were two to do it. To do it is to say goodbye forever to warm days, sunny fellowship, the ease that glowed briefly between us now. Each lost in our gathering languages, our friends our words, devoted to loneliness, as to love itself. Going always from that to which there is most attachment in order to come again. He is London. I am Ireland. No other way. Each by absence giving the other presence, but he having the best of it. Me the one to say the division which it was my (foul? foiled? fake?) ambition to heal. I, the healer, wanting to widen the rift; he, no healer at all, having no desire to do other than to outline the problem and its ghostly origin, wanting to close it.

We exchanged not a single word.

XII

"THE SKY WAS a deep, impossible blue. And the sea was absolutely still, also blue but with a tinge of green. The water's expanse was motionless, a plane of glossy quiet. We were becalmed. Not the faintest breeze to ruffle the sails. To starboard was the coast of Africa, no more than a hundred yards distant. We would not set ashore for fear of savages."

The Queen was speaking, telling me of her other dream. I had been summoned at my lodgings by special messenger, who seemed to have dressed in black for the part. I was to come at night this time. When the day's business was over. I was in her bedchamber which was remarkably sparsely furnished. An ornate bed of state, yes, but apart from this the cedar boards of the bedroom were bare. In one corner stood a washstand on which was a pitcher and dish. The room was lit by candles.

"Madam, what part did you have in this dream?"

"I was the sea-captain, I think. Our purpose wasn't clear. A voyage of fortune or a mapping expedition, it doesn't matter. We were there, off the west coast of Africa, no stir of wind for days, and we were afraid to go ashore. Sometimes we would see the savages watching us. A number of them would sometimes scurry back into hiding after they had come out to watch when there had been no one on deck. Sometimes we could see one or two of them in the trees, hidden by the thick growth of the tropical forest. At times the scent of vegetation would come offshore, though there were no breezes to carry it. The men were getting restless; one in particular was for going ashore to find drink and women, but I resisted him. It took every nerve, every fibre of my brain, but I knew I had to. Had he managed to best me in the argument he would have had the party ashore and he would never have been seen again. He was derisive about the dangers, but I knew the fearsomeness of the coast, how many hundreds of ships had disappeared just at this spot, these small doldrums. At the horizon's edge we could see activity: clouds coming and going, a grey turbulence of rain; while here all was sunshine, beating down mercilessly, and the silent watchers from the shore day and night. Sometimes at the dead of night we could hear the sound of drums coming from far inland, and those nearer shore replying. Talking of us. Those drums, Spenser; they spoke and yelled, shifting their notes in mid-tone. They were like creatures of the forest itself. In any case I talked the restless one out of his resolve but I still had a problem. How was I to keep the crew from lunacy, from throwing themselves into the warm, shark-infested sea, driven mad by heat and lethargy, and swimming to death onshore at the hands of those dark cannibals?

"Sitting in my cabin one day, idling through some books, I came across an old play by, I think, Kyd, called *Hamlet*. I thought it would amuse the crew if we could mount it in these doldrums. I selected the main actors and very quickly (you know how time speeds up in dreams) we were in performance. Again, an airless, unbearably hot day. We set up a canopy from spare sails under which we were to act out our play. I was to play Hamlet's mother, whose father, the old king, also called Hamlet, had been killed by his brother, now my husband. The reckless one who wanted to go ashore I got to play the prince, and I got an old croaking senior from Yarmouth to play the ghost who tells his tale of woe to the young prince at the beginning of the play. That is the scene I remember most: old Hamlet, old Guttridge from Yarmouth, darkly telling the young prince, played by Tompkins, of his murder. A piece of sailcloth was hung across the near corner of our covered area, behind which old Guttridge stood proclaiming his direful tale. Tompkins was acting like a man possessed, as if this story had gone into him, this tale of blood, poison and incest. He turned on me, eyes blazing, departing from Kyd's script and, levelling his gaze at me said (I remember all, or nearly all of these

words – these, Spenser, are not old groaner Kyd's: they are
Tompkins's own in my dream):

Bitch, prick-eater, man-charger,
What filth you do to us in your serene silences,
Your preenings and struttings.
Each action of each limb,
Each tremble of an eyelid a searching out
Of whatever antagonism is possible
That may in the end kill us all.
Your kind want us to bear witness
Against ourselves, against ourselves,
So that we can develop in our heads
A tightening constriction, ever straitening,
That will in the end explode,
Laying waste all our gathered interests
All our carefully worked elaborateness
Making the whole world a bowl of flames.
That is the fire you want above all fires,
That is the flame you want to leap out of your eyes
Ripping into our groins, searing every privacy
Of limb and eye and socket
With your thunderous strangeness.
Galvanisers of our forlorn angers,
When what we kill always is ourselves
Driven by you, driven by you.
We will for a time banish you,
And watch your thatch of hair crackle in a pyre
In a city square, but you will at last
Come back, strengthened by all our evasions,

Fortified by avoidances, to insinuate
That all our doings all along
Were the wronging of you, when we also,
In ourselves, were wronging those selves.
Even our vehemence of lust you will destroy
Taking it apart through the confidence
That is expert in inflicting remorse.

"Tompkins ran out of speech. In his silence I filled with pride. He had given himself away. I had him. I looked around and I saw on shore a hundred blacks or more, all gathered, silent, looking at the white people dressed up in strange clothes (I was draped in a sailcloth; Tompkins in a suit of black). When I turned around, they moved back and, slowly, slunk back into the dark shade of the tropical forest. I had a feeling that we were as them, standing revealed occasionally, but shifting back into cover as soon as we notice we are in the open, uncovered. Us, white cannibals, dishonest, failing in speech, like Tompkins, Spenser, or like you, or me. Even when the situation comes when it might be possible to stand revealed we try to find a way back in rodomontade, speechifying, never standing the ground. Those black ones, Spenser, those black eaters of human flesh, were just as you and I, consuming each other in the guise of listening. Can you taste my flesh?"

I was appalled.

"No, Madam, I protest. You go too far. If you think such things, how can you govern?"

"It is because I know such things that I do govern. But it

74

is only a holding action, as you yourself would say. Have said."

She knew as clearly as I did what was in store. And she knew how I thought, how with one half of me, or more than half, I welcomed the collapse, the suffering, the exclusion, because that was how our fate as a species was to be decided. It was all to come out. There was nothing for it now.

"Madam, the Africa you sailed off in your dreams must out. In that play of Kyd's you were rehearsing it, practising for what will come out in the laws of fortune, chance and destiny. Tompkins wore black, because he was, in the play, of Africa. That's why he wanted to swim ashore. And the prince he played is prince of darkest Africa, the nameless confusion in us all, the dark haunted by our fathers' failed strength, our mothers' thwarted gentleness. It is in that dark we come to be, it is our duty to bring that into a semblance of rule so the semblance may take hold and live in joy. But is it not possible that the bleak phase of black vehemence and hatred, that Tompkins let go, is it not possible that that too will pass and another phase develop? That is what I, as writer, am trying to be about, though usually I try to put more optimistic constructions on the whole affair. I cast the dance into one hopeful attitude of grace. But the material is always escaping, will always escape from constructions of hope, or from those other ones just as deceitful, that revel in dolefulness."

"Would that statesmen could find ways of bringing your clarity of vision into practice, but of course their talents are different. All semblances and resemblances, and" (she was laughing now) "they all get to look alike at last. Do they not?"

At that moment I loved her.

XIII

SOME DISTANCE FROM my house here in Kilcolman there is a grove formed naturally by the hazels, through which it is possible to go if you crouch down, avoiding the thin branches, red and vicious. It is there that I have set my tale of "The Parting", which I had hoped to bring into my poem, but I am not sure how it may be done. It is a tale which, if I succeed in finding images for it, will be a source of great relief and ease to many, as when the pain is open and recognised, no longer hidden in the labyrinth of the flesh that disguises everything, but out, declared, raging into its full manic intensity, clenching the body so that it has to recognise, to own up. Pain is clarity. It is relief.

It goes like this: he and she, those two, have to come there in an afternoon of heat and silence. The hazels are in full leaf and the ground underneath is covered with a mast of old leaves and decayed kernels, now altered into an aromatic carpet. The afternoon is to be given over to love. They have been planning this space for themselves for a long time, years possibly, years full of business, and the incessant following of children from one room to another. All is well. Officially all going to plan. Except. Except their two minds which in this case contain two quite separate awarenesses, thoughts, pictures, whatever. (This is going to be difficult. Am I the man to do this?) In her case it is a large snake-like creature, save that (ridiculous) instead of wriggling along the ground with the swift muscular adaptiveness of the serpent, this one hops along, using the rear half of the body as a rubbery form of propulsion, that flexes and unflexes. He moves very swiftly through the undergrowth in her mind in this odd form of locomotion. The creature is about four foot high. In the man's mind a woman stands over him, facing away from him, her legs clad in the finest black mesh, slowly lowering it from her two cheeks. She turns toward him and lewdly purses her lips, reddened and glistening with cosmetic. Her eyes are shaded green. The fingers working in the black mesh fascinate, their tips a fiery red. She wears shoes with elongated heels that help arch her legs and bring out the elaborately beautiful co-ordination of muscle and ligament under the mesh, that second flesh not of skin. (Ridiculous, ridiculous, but I must go on.) He tries to tell her what he is thinking, but his tongue cannot say the words. There are no words for what he wants to say. It is so obvious, but he is frightened. She, on the other side, is troubled by the immensity of this absurd jumping lump of rubber which makes her laugh. This strikes him like a blow which she feels more than he does in the distance that has started to grow between them.

She tells him she wishes to be alone in another part of the hazel copse, but cannot say why. It is the ludicrousness of that flexing length of rubbery motion and the forlornness she feels in having no option but to think of it. He, on his side, is both relieved and disappointed by her need for solitude. When she goes now, he thinks, she goes forever. He tries to persuade her to stay with him but he cannot organise enough conviction to lend strength to his speech.

"Don't you know that your place is by my side this time, now of all times?"

Losing her even as he was saying it. Stridency advancing. Loss. No persuading what is at odds. Only coercion after that. No knowing what brutalities issue from their division. She wants to leave the enclosure of the copse, the quiet romantic grove lit greenly by the leaves brightened by the sunlight. Her long hair tangling slightly with some stray branches of hazel, she turns a little to detach the tendrils. Intent on this small operation, her face looks peaceful, stronger, as she goes from him. All their conversations hereafter would be nervous, embarked on in the hope of sharing, not out of the assurance of belonging.

Not far from the copse, at the summit of the hill on

which it stood, a wall, and a gate of pearl. Inside the wall a garden with intersecting paths of fine circular stones. At each junction a statue or a fountain. Stillness or the splash of water. Couples moved two by two along the pathways or on the grass between them holding hands. Their progressions were orderly and harmonious though each couple had their own special pattern. All were governed by the white temple that occupied the centre of the garden. Inside, a gloomy peace. A series of circular sanctuaries until at the mid-point of all a turning dais around which was draped a green veil. Behind it (and this was only shown to those who had the privilege to live within the temple itself) the roseate terror of the hermaphrodite deity, breasts and hair, vagina and phallus. In the right hand it held the cross of Christ fashioned in black ivory, in its left a livid green serpent wriggled, its scales shining. Blood ran from the tiny figure on the cross down the clenched elevated arm of the half-man half-woman.

This story will be better told by one who is to come after me, one for whom all his life's meaning will clarify in these scenes. I can even envisage him: black-clothed, blind, his breath stale from too continuous strife. In his cabinet of an afternoon he composes long stretches of verse, ungoverned Latinity, each blaze of words a blow, striking at some enemy or himself, raving in the dim light. Why is he so isolated, doomed to those blazing sentences? His speech a special mask to put on his head. A contraption with black holes for eyes. A down-turned mouth, insisting on its gravity. Inside this great wooden head a complexity of small hollows all of different volume, so that each intonation of the voice was mixed, variegated, deepened into many tones. Multi-speech. The slightest sound would set the whole interior singing. A sentence would replay itself to itself many times, so that grammatical progression, while not stilled, was prolonged, in the scrutiny of the interior. Booming away to himself in his discreet cabinet, this man of many tones. Narcissus of Liberty. Each man his own episcopate. This man, I, a Merlin, saw before his time.

XIV

THE PRINTING OF my book was going reasonably well. The stanzas looked well on the heavy paper: black lines of order imposed on vacancy. I liked to think that the paper onto which my rhymes were slammed by the machines were Irish timber, dried out, refined and marked by our technology. Ireland's woody fastnesses brought to book. The printer was an affable sort with one eye and a gammy leg, who had been at Zutphen. His nickname was Gangrene. He had the sunny disposition of the maimed who survive.

I would take the proof sheets and go to Raleigh with them sometimes. He would walk up and down the polished sea-boards of his room, intoning the stanzas gracelessly in his Devonshire accent.

"You've done it, Spunse, old spunk. You've brought it off. You'll give that old shite Tasso something to think about at his evening devotions. This is the answer to those over-weening weenies down in Spain. I can just see Don Phillipino's mustachio trembling with rage; that lying rat with his shining teeth."

His enthusiasm would always depress me. It reduced things to an inert desert. I felt subdued by it, outlawed. When he would go on about Don Phillipino The Weeno (as he called him) I'd be the Spaniard in my own mind. I'd be Raleigh's laughing post. In these outbursts occasioned by my verse, I would find myself hating him.

XV

THE QUEEN HAD said that there was to be another dream session. I was summoned on an afternoon in April. When I got to her private apartment, the same one in which we had had the first session, she was in a plain white shift, without any make-up, and her wig was off. She was very nearly bald. Her stomach, ungirdled, swelled out under the shift, distended, I am sure, by some digestive disorder. Even from the doorway I could get the fetid stink of her decaying body.

I remember my father telling me, in his crude accent, stories of the stinking trunk of her father. "Like England," he used to say. "Like England. They smell of power and money. Acquire that stink, Ned. Acquire the odour of expensive corruption."

I haven't. Not through the want of trying. But enough of that.

She was distressed and had been crying. She looked like a widow in a hovel on my estate at Kilcolman after she has been told that, with her husband gone, she must leave and take her children with her.

But this regal, childless crone – what had I to do with her? This red bloated face, gummy eyes, bald head?

"This is our last session, Spenser; I am very glad you have taken the trouble to come like this and hear my trouble. After our conversation I have taken the liberty of arranging for us some private entertainment, which I hope will be to your taste."

"I am sure, Madam."

"Enough. We begin."

She moved to her seat opposite the window, under the soft tints of the painting. Her face became blank and expressionless. In the moments before she began to talk a thrill of excitement, despair, or perhaps it might be better termed a sense of implication, started to work in my stomach and bowels. Again a sense of a pain located, its source opened to the probe, the small intricacy of the structure which has gone awry. Crying out for correcting. She spoke.

"A woman in a hovel in a damp country with a child at her breast. Her man, a poet, has left to find work in the city. It is called Corcach, the marsh, the swampland. Her other children have died of starvation. With great difficulty she has buried them, all five of them, in a circle around the heap of wattle which is their dwelling on an island in the middle of a mere-like lake. The lake is about a day's journey from the city. It is winter. Cold January weather.

"The dream moves back to the summer, when hopes were still high that her man would come back. On warm days the children would catch fish – trout, salmon, sometimes the huge snouting pike – from the tufts of grass-covered earth that dotted the lake when it was not in flood. In summer it was possible for a man to get ashore leaping from one tussock to another and she would often tell the older children – Mícheál, Dáibhí, Sybil, Nóra – to look out for their father: that they would be seeing him leaping from the shore, a huge sack on his back from Cork, carrying in it playthings for them, and a rattle for little Seosamh, then only two months old. There would be a large cake covered in almonds, which they would eat together looking over the water, and he would tell them of his adventures in the city: how he did meet the Bishop, in the end, who asked him to do the big Codex of the saints of Ireland. And that Éilís herself, the great golden Queen in London, who had stars for eyes, wanted him to write the entire history of *Éire Chuinn* in Irish; that she wished to learn the language and know her subjects better. The stories which came through about the great Queen's good will and kindness all were true. Was it not just good sense for her to love her Irish subjects? No, the stories that her teeth were made of black iron, and that her stomach was afire with hatred of the Irish – this was all invention. Was it not better to be her loyal subjects than to be under the whim of the dirty tyrants here at home? Their father was a sensible man, she would tell them, and had worked all this out for himself, and deduced that what Éilís's man in Cork would want, above all things, was someone who could supply him with reliable information, about Éire and her past, how, genealogically and poetically it was a simple matter to install Éilís in the Irish mind as *Mór Ríoghan na hÉireann*, the Great Queen of Ireland. And in any case, there was the Bishop, who would want the Codex.

"As she would talk to them, in the deepening summer haze, her limbs would fill with a sluggish sleepy happiness. All was well. Her man was a great genius, and a kind father, attentive to his responsibilities towards his children. She loved him so much, and loved him through the little ones. Her eyes swam with tears of peace as she looked at their faces turned towards the shore, their hearts singing at the thought that at any moment their father would come leaping from the shore carrying with him oranges, dates and the almond cake from Cork.

"But as the year darkened and the weather got colder they did not look so much. One by one they died. Mícheál, the oldest and strongest, was the first to go. He did without his food, save for a few scraps, so the little ones would not go hungry. She had tried to explain to him that it was stupid, that his strength was needed most of all, for without him they would find it hard to catch the few fish on which they now entirely relied. They buried him on a blustery day at the end of November. With him gone, the others lost heart. Sybil disappeared one night. She must have tried to swim ashore, but the lake was in flood and she could not have made it. Dáibhí and Nóra died in one night, clung together for warmth. Their cheeks had frozen together in the cot. She did not disentangle them from their last embrace, but put them in the grave together, as they were, their arms wrapped around each other. She left their grave shallow, knowing that she would be putting little Seosamh in after them. She hoped that when the weather improved, and when the dog packs came (of which there were a great many all over Munster this last year) they might be satisfied with the remnants of her decayed corpse and her bones, and that they would leave the last shallow grave alone, and depart, howling, for the meatier pastures further up the valley. They had chosen the lake dwelling as a refuge because it was little known and would be safe from the marauders, human and animal, that always roam the country in times of famine.

"Now the dream moves back to where it opened, and she is sitting on a smooth stone inside the cabin on the island. It is January and Seosamh, the little one, is taking the last few drops from her shrivelled dugs.

"The withered ferns, that in brighter days had acted as a shade in the aperture in the wall that served as a window, shook briefly in a slight movement of wind. Coming across the grey water was a black barge-like vessel with two men labouring at clumsy oars. In the prow stood a knight at arms in black armour, a red cross on a white background emblazoned on his chest. His visor was down. His face all metal. The barge sank into the muddy silt of the shore and the knight at arms leapt on to land, extraordinarily agile for a man in full armour.

"He made straight for the hovel and smashed right through the wattle door Mícheál had spent two days making, drawing his sword as he came through. A white plume poured out of the grille of his helmet at each exhalation. Seeing the woman with the child he pulled the baby from her breast by one leg. It wailed, thinly. He, lifting it up, raised it to shoulder height and brought the sword down between its two legs, cutting the body perfectly in half. He threw the piece he held against the wall. Each side of the body had a testicle, so neat and sure was the stroke.

"Then he turned to her, the mother. 'My name,' he said, 'is Justice.' She spoke to him, but did not plead or beg; what she said was in Irish, which he did not understand. There was a softness in the air between them, a collusion. Her pain was purifying him. The first blow of the sword slammed into her head, but did not fell her.

"'*Arís*,' she said. '*Gread leat agus mill tú féin*.'* A slow sense of triumph in her voice, even joy.

"The next blow was into the side of the neck and it went right into her chest bone, where it stuck.

"'So easy,' he said, 'so easy.'

"He held her up by the sword for a moment, before yanking the blade out of her chest. She fell. He lifted the visor and went out of the hovel. Two blue eyes scoured the rest of the island, noticing five wooden crosses arranged in a circle around the dwelling. His eyes watered when he realised that he would never be free of this place. She had

*"*Again," she said. "Go on and destroy yourself.*"

him. That hovel was to be the place he would always come to in secrecy and guilt, looking for the furtive sharing.

"That, Spenser, is the last dream I am going to burden you with."

Again I had the sense that the meanings of these things were pressing on me. I longed to be at Kilcolman, free of the stress of trouble, evident in her disarray, the confusion in her mind, that made her seek out the likes of me, and in the elaborateness of the life that moved around her. I knew now that I was finished in that city; it was a place to get my books printed up, that was all. But, again, why did I share this woman's dreams? Her story, which filled me with an impossible sadness and sterile agitation, spoke to me of the dereliction that is especially mine, that I must look to, and, if I can, mend.

I knew I was going to have to talk, to perform, and I felt silenced, numbed. I did not understand the import of that dream to myself, let alone to the Queen of England, haughty empress, blubber-eyed from crying.

"Madam, your dream, I confess, I have some familiarity with."

She stared.

"I have had the same dream, or at least nearly the same dream, on the trip from Ireland when I was bringing over my manuscript of *The Faerie Queene*. And I have to say that it baffles me. It has to do, no doubt, with Ireland, and with your royal attitude and your policies towards her; it seems to have something to do with Lord Grey's methods of dealing with the Munster rebellion, and the subsequent famine. But in my dream, and in yours, there seems to be a

90

mutual exchange of fate between the aggressor and the victim, the knight and the mother with her starving babes.

"It seems to me that you have nothing to feel guilty of, nor have I, or we, as English. It is a law that human nature will not easily submit itself to rule. We, who wish to bring peace to our globe, must be prepared to be resolute in justice: we must have an iron man inside us, otherwise those whom we wish to subdue will know our insecurity for sure, and their knowing will be our undoing."

I was warming to my subject. To hell with honesty.

"What can they accuse us of? They accuse us in the name of Human Kindness, Sympathy, Common Humanity, other such. Give me one of these pleaders, let me open up his heart (as a poet that is my function, Madam), and let us see where all these virtues are by which he made his stern appeal. What shall we find? We'll find Self-Interest, The Look Out for the Main Chance, and simple Greed. Give me a pleader and I will give you his opposite. So fear not the accusers: by virtue of the accusations you know them to be false. Is there a single heart that can call on the name of a single virtue and so declare himself by her light? The answer is surely no.

"But what then can govern behaviour? By what means may justice be administered? There are two answers to this: one is the light bestowed on us by Christ himself in the Gospels; the other is that nothing can govern behaviour: there is no true administration of justice."

"What use is this, Master Spenser? This is riddling."

"It is all I can come up with. Would you have preferred me to say that you, Madam, were yourself the light by

91

which we see the means to decide between conflicting opposites; that you were the equanimity that abides in certainty at the centre?"

"No," she replied, "I should not have preferred you to say that, but you should have done so nonetheless. But which side do you favour? Do you see the light as triumphant or is it that there is no administration of government, no order, no cohesion?"

"I cannot answer that, Madam. I cannot. But I suspect that the resolute arm, lifted to strike, is prevented by many things, among them love and kindness, hate and dismay, self-contempt and self-admiration. The knight in the dream can say to himself that he is acting according to his duty, but there is always a thrill of pleasure along the groin, an excitement, even at the thought of the sensuality the full depth of his remorse will bring to him in later years."

"You are a Puritan, Master Spenser."

"Can you deny the truth of what I say? There is no natural goodness."

"You lie and you know you lie. Being, over which I preside, is good. Our evil ways are our evil ways, but our evil does not touch that core of good."

"And you, Madam, I fear, are something of a Papist."

"You grow into too great a liberty, but I forgive you. You have been encouraged, and you are soon to return to the silence of your Cork estates. But Spenser, what of that woman and her children?"

A stab of pain ran through me, from my left ear to my groin.

"Their grief will live forever."

"Has such cruelty been done in Ireland?"

"Yes."

"It must be put to rights."

"How?"

"The knaves who visited such atrocities must be seized and put to death."

"Those knaves, Madam, were those acting on your explicit instructions. And those who would bring them to task? What of them? They, too, would enter into the atrocity. There is no punishment once the evil is out. Only further cruelty driving the wrong deeper and wider."

"Puritan gnomons," she said, snorting derisively. And maybe she was right. I, whose estates all owe to such injustices and severity, advocating non-interference. A complex conscience: is that the last ditch of the greedy fearful?

"Madam, I do not know. I think there may be something in what I've said, but no one can be more conscious of his worthlessness than I; my frivolity and rhetorical laziness. I know I go off into foolish talk and I hardly know what I'm going to say before I've said it. Forgive me."

"You are not forgiven. It is, friend Spenser, time for the entertainment. Come."

XVI

B Y NOW IT was late afternoon. As we left the room
and went through the door (not the one leading
back out to the room of state) I glanced at her
face. The puffiness had gone. A cold majesty had returned. Now she was moving with abrupt serenity. She
was out there away from me again, and I a (temporarily)
favoured subject. I was uneasy, filled with a sense of
foolishness, and again I wanted to be away from there. But
I had to go through with this afternoon, this entertainment, whatever it was.

We passed down a corridor, the walls of which were
shrouded in green velvet, the floor a mosaic of black-and-
white polished stone tiles, set diagonally. A manservant

passed, arrayed in white. He was a blackamoor. A spicy smell rode past us on the air as he saluted and stole softly by. I was in the notorious pleasure apartments of the palace, much talked about, greatly feared. I had heard it said once that here the Queen could change herself into a man, that she kept specimens from all over the globe with which to amuse herself when oppressed by affairs. Nowhere more than in Ireland do these rumours attain fantastic extremes and most elaborate barbarities.

Passing quietly through these hushed corridors I thought of the abominations the Irish clerics would be inventing for her in Salamanca or Louvain: that here she kept a pack of Arctic foxes trained to pleasure her diabolically; that she had a servant with a tongue a foot long. And so on. Her strange bearing, her elastic confidence, would now seem to give credence to these wild stories.

"You do realise, Master Spenser, that not many of my subjects are favoured in the way that you are favoured now. Not many see my inner world, my privacy. In here all may be realised, all complexity catered for."

"Fathomed?" I ventured, falteringly.

"That is a different matter. To arrange a show, a play, an enactment is one thing; to fathom – well, that is another. We leave fathoming to sailors, poets and play-wrights. Let you fathom whether what you see and feel is indeed a fathoming. Though I doubt if it will be."

We passed into a chamber off the corridor, in which was set a door. She opened this and went through. As soon as we were inside some elaborate contraption turned on a system of concealed lighting, which lit the room softly. I could scarcely believe it: it was the sea-cave of my dream and of hers. The lights were greenish blue; the walls were made to look as if they were great sheering vaults of rock; the floor, covered with fine white sand, was strewn with seaweed and shells. Precious stones gleamed, half-hidden, here and there in the sand.

At the far wall there was a couch with a system of thongs and leg-straps. The Queen gestured to me that I should lie down upon it. She was smiling now, and kindly. The vague light half-concealed her wasted features and she managed to look whorish.

"Please take your position, Master Spenser, for the entertainment. It is called 'The Humiliation' and I had this room specially designed for it. A man's disgrace is good for him, when conducted in private. It lends assurance to his public poise. When you hear the confident roar of one of my statesmen, know that what lends that roar authority is the private place of shame I have set aside for them all in these chambers. They shout, impelled by delight at the thought of the disgrace renewed at these hands" (holding them up) "and at the hands of my assistants."

At this a girl appeared from behind one of the shelves of rock, dressed in a light green gown, which clung to her body. She walked delicately across the sandy floor, each step cautiously taken because she was wearing very high Venetian heels. Her face was heavily painted with green and blue, and her lips were darkened with a black cosmetic. She came up and murmured something into the

Queen's ear, then they both disappeared back to where the girl had come from. By now I was lying on the couch. The Queen came out and fastened the straps around my ankles and one around my neck. The girl re-appeared carrying a tangle of leather thongs and belts. Again she and the Queen murmured together, but I did overhear one phrase:

"It is time for him to grow up."

I had started to sweat. The girl came over and, lifting up my doublet, sliced it open with a sharp knife in one clean stroke. The Queen came over and fastened a further belt around my midriff.

"We will leave you now for a few moments," she said. "Let your fear anticipate whatever you most fear, most desire."

They left. Silence in the chamber, except for the soft hiss of the lights, powered by some source that I could not understand. Vacancy. A grey scene filled my mind. A city street. Railings around an area of soggy green. Opposite a bookshop. The streets mostly empty. Those who were on the streets dressed in outlandish clothes, in keeping with the greyness.

The Queen and her assistant came back dressed in tight black suits. They both wore boots with perilously high heels and their waists were cinched with wide red belts. Over their eyes they wore black half-masks. The girl carried a small whip with a number of thongs. At the tip of each there sparkled a tiny burr of bright metal. Without warning she strode over and slashed into my chest with the whip. A clot of agony gathered in my breast as the burrs bit into the skin. Blood poured out of five tiny wounds.

"Let me explain," the Queen said. "It is necessary that you suffer thus. Once the physical agony has been gone through in private like this, at the hands of experts like ourselves, then you no longer feel the sense of waste, oppression, uselessness, with which your mind fills; you are released through real terror, real suffering, real feeling. Feel again."

Again the lash descended, this time on the stomach, and again five points of blood opened up. I had, unbelievably, started to get an erection. I looked at the long legs of the girl, the tightly fitting suit, the high heels and cinched waist, and I found her ravishing. When she moved the tight leather moved along her sleek flank. She seemed high, remote, beautiful.

"The knife, Madam," she said to the Queen. "We have the usual insolence in the codpiece."

I gasped. The Queen came over and neatly ripped open my codpiece. My member started up into the cool air. They chortled with glee. And then, slowly, fiercely, with real relish and deliberate savagery, the girl brought the lash down on my genitals. I passed out.

XVII

THE DARK AND faces sliding by. Raleigh's, mine. Under a shelf of rock, the black eminence above me. I am so small in this greatness. It moves and pulses to a huge swinging rhythm. Undersea. Undersea.

XVIII

A BEDROOM. A WOMAN stood by the bedside, in the act of removing a system of straps from around her breasts. Her waist was encircled by a tight white article of underwear. But it was her flesh which appalled me. It was white but under the skin the complicated network of veins was apparent, so that one had the sense of seeing the interior of the surface.

"Hello, fuckface," she said.

As I passed a mirror, moving more fully into the room, I caught a glimpse of my face, which was so pained and tightened that it had altered out of all recognition. At the base of each cheek stood a knot of muscle, hard and thin.

"Pain has done this to you," she said. "You have been

too long pained and distressed. So hard for you, so hard."
She moved towards me and clutched at my genitals. My
penis awoke. She was beautiful, despite the appallingly
intricate configurations on her skin. Her hair was blond
and fell over her face as she bent down in a lewd caress.
She shook it back and she looked into my eyes.

"Fuck me," she said. She climbed onto the bed and,
staying on all fours, offered me her rear. I went over and
caressed that smooth roseate warmth, admiring the curves
and the cleft which contained the two secrecies now
exposed to my view. The cinch on her waist seemed to
make her buttocks more pronounced. I sank my member
in, holding her by the flanks. It moved into the secret
warmth, slowly, sensing every corrugation in that interior.
It seemed as if my penis had gathered an intense heat into
itself. I drew it out again, slowly, allowing the head just to
nestle against the orifice for a time, fully enjoying the
tantalising effect I was having on myself.

"Please," she said, "put it in again. Just an inch."

Slowly again I worked it in, feeling the strained tension
in her muscles under my hands. I sank it in. Running my
hands around the front of her body I touched her breasts
on the points. She winced. A spurt of heat met my member
as I reached full penetration. All my loins shuddered
internally and a searing heat passed along my member to
join her depth.

I awoke to find the Queen's assistant straddled over me,
one leg at each side of my body, writhing up and down on
my flaccid penis.

"So you saw the Rosy Queen?" It was the Queen's

101

voice, speaking from a dark corner. When I looked harder I could see her sitting, looking at the girl pleasuring herself.

"Can I go?" I asked.

"Yes, but we shall, of course, never see each other again. You've seen the Rosy Queen. You've seen who I am. Once that has happened you can never see me again. If ever you try to gain audience with me you will be assassinated. I can have anyone assassinated anywhere in Europe, in America, even in Africa. You cannot escape me."

Walking home that night I longed for Ireland. Kilcolman's sunny days, when peace might seem as if it never would stop; where I dig my garden, planting flowers and shrubs, the work growing lighter as the wildness is tamed. Oh such a profound sadness not to be there; knowing, too, that when I am there I shall be heart-struck by the thoughts of all this here in London, all the filth, antagonism, the violence that galvanises dreams, all that being missed. And I, a monster, hate what I adore.

Three days later I sailed to Ireland.

XIX

ON BOARD SHIP in my cabin, its rough wooden walls giving off the odour of resin in the heat. Through the small round window the blue sky. A light breeze as the ship rocks lightly. London fading away, becoming unreal. How deeply I had grown to love the place which at first I so abhorred. Thinking of the warm fire at Kilcolman after a winter's day out surveying the land, deciding what to plant the coming year, talking to my sickleman with the missing thumb. He saying that I made good sense.

Now. Family, my dear wife, commitments. Such anxiety. But there is this scribbling. This keeps me in touch. How I have longed for language. All those confections and hurryings, those fits, epileptic striving for nuance, only to find it turgid at the end.

There is one who comes to me, infrequently. An importunate. With grey hair flowing over a clear forehead. All his vice controlled (not me, not me). He comes at night along a projectile from the future. A lank enquiry. But I know he'll not desist until the answer corresponds to the strike of the question:

"Is it worth all this effort based upon denial?" he asks. "Are you not pornographer royal, mean exploiter of the inner desert of your time, giving it mirages of luxury, offering it the softness of delusion, that keeps you from thoughtful vigour? You do not like the flesh you try with your depiction. Vanishings, vanishings. Is it not true that you failed to make a speech that the body could be easy in; and is it not so that we, that is, those of us condemned to speech, should contrive such a language? Make the speech a place for the body to be at home in. Look what your opposite and rival, Shakespeare, did when all was frozen into nothingness and misinterpretation at Elsinore. What did he do? He brought the players in, the players with their body-speech tumbling into the frozen circle where the mind has petrified speech; he brings in the players, with striped jerkins and strangeness, and makes them jump. That is, my friend, the leap of harmony and relationship. You, Pensivo, are the darkened tedium of laborious progression."

I do not know who this is, of course. I know he is from Ireland, of the future, and I know he is a danger to me. He is preceded by a pale-faced girl with tight auburn curls.

104

When she comes my head fills with the scent of apple-blossom. I feel so lost when she is come and I know his insistent questioning is a danger to my resolve. When he comes, in dreams, it is days before I can summon courage to begin to write again.

XX

TO EMBARK.

On board ship, in my cabin, I was staring vacantly at the boards in my ceiling, admiring the craftsmanship, especially at the corners where the timber was dovetailed to the walls to keep them secure. I was drifting to sleep when two voices began to speak.

"He is no man."

"Not to be trusted, no."

"Marlowe said he had those tendencies."

"Yes, but with Marlowe you must be cautious."

"O'Neill's our man for fate."

"You mean, to keep the fate of Ireland secure to itself?"

"Yes. Encourage him to distrust and violence and that is all that is necessary. His temperament will do the rest."

"And how do we do that?"

"We do that by agreeing with everything O'Neill says. Even if he asks for the removal of the Queen's deputy, we agree to it. The Irish do not have the temperament for affairs. They cannot hold back, entering, as they do, the complexity of a situation with their whole minds. That is how they are fucked. What we must never do is really sympathise. If we do we are no use to them, to ourselves, to the Queen, to anything. We must keep ourselves sane and free, and through that we may bring them to sanity and freedom, but there must be no loose sympathising. O'Neill must be encouraged into the restlessness of his active temperament."

"Which they all have?"

"Yes, all. There isn't one of them free of it. Wait long enough and the coldest of them joins the rest, howling in distress, pleading to be understood, vicious. And then roaring, snarling, rising into the dignity of loss and rage, vowing to have our heads, saying that they will feed our livers to their brats. They're good at that. Vehemence."

"What of our Undertakers?* Master Spenser and the like?"

"They are the buriers of the dead and they themselves are dead."

"How do you mean?"

*Colonists who "undertook" to settle on land seized after the Munster Rebellion.

107

"They are dead because they have gone out of the life that is theirs, into strangeness. They give their lives for something, and they never quite know what. That is why they are also so damn serious and unbending. They have the aspect of Christ. They become unfit for life in England, growing to abhor what is most dear, to love what is most strange. They actually begin to become affectionate about that ludicrous country with its bogs and lakes and dreary monotonous mountains, a country without scenery or variety. And this is their undoing, because no one takes them seriously any longer. They are hated by the courtiers, whom they stir to a resentment which increases the more they profess to have formed a common cause or sympathy with the aborigines."

"And this, you say, is a vital element in our policy?"

"Of course, because the more attached they become to the land, the more the courtiers are roused to fury by them. O'Neill and his like detest ambiguity, and Spenser and his like are ambiguous from the very depth of their being. This is why we send intellectuals on these colonial enterprises. Their ambiguity and susceptibility create the dissension that allows scope."

"And that scope is necessary to us, because? Well, is it because in it we keep ourselves under control?"

"Yes; we master our Irishness by mastering the Irish. Life is all the same. We master our blackness by mastering black Africa. There is no other way."

"So the state, then, is dominance?"

"Yes. That is how it is effective.

"Each small victory ensures the free play of our

intelligence. But it must be thoughtless. No thought must enter that carries with it the weight of thinking. That is absolutely useless. Our speech must be galvanic, bright, alert, inventive, sharp."

"None of Spenser's pensiveness, then?"

"No, that is for the infuriation of the natives, the perturbation of the peace. We *say*, of course, that Master Spenser is to keep the peace, but really what we want is trouble, and the greater the disaster the better. Who isn't pleased with the news of brutality?"

Tears filled my eyes. They are there now. In my nose and throat. Thinking of the brave men at Dunanore, bright Spaniards; carrying with them the cross of Christ, smashed down by the cannonade of the black English guns. The balls of iron screaming in the dark air. Seas lurching. The swords hacking at the bodies even when they were prostrate. Gutting and disembowelling, having fun with the Catholic tripes. One whey-faced soldier, looking to my lord's approval, a heart on the point of his sword, the valves still spurting, clots of blood on his beard, as he licks his lips, shouting: "The blood of Christ, the blood of Christ!"

When will my country be? When will it be free?

I wept in the room, aromatic with the scent of resin, for myself and for Christ. And, shockingly, searingly, for Ireland. My country. My home. My people in their rags and dirt and filth. Their bad teeth and stinking breath; their ludicrous speech; their hopelessness. There was relief in crying. A curious peace settled on my mind. I was now a native, even though I could never be accepted. Cut off from England by the Queen's confidences, I was now part of that other life over there across the sea. I was an undertaker, surveying the dead, but with love. With love. Unreturned, unrecognised, rejected love.

The dead I was burying England could never forget. I am undertaker of the centre of her life even though I was out there on the edge. Shovelling the silt to make way for the many requiring oblivion, that the palace may glitter on the waves, surviving.

A slow thought filled my head. An interlude of profound terror. A poet in a dirty white coat, sitting at a table, his hand inside his breeches, fondling himself. The word "peruke" floated in the air, tickling his left ear. He had a hunch on his back. To the left of the table a small silver pan upon a tripod, in which lamprey fried slowly, in butter. A stink of melted fat and soft fish. A long pipe lay to the right of his writing pad. He was trying to describe the movement of sludge, dimpling on the Thames. He had slowed down the course of the river in his mind to a sluggish ooze, in which poets dived and swam. Underneath, the British nymphs gorged on great turds of shit, swimming blissfully through the semi-solid murk, eyes closed, enjoying the mild collision of the turds against their white bodies. An underground sewage system added to the piquancy of their medium by contri-buting from Hampton Court a tributary of pure piss, warm and aromatic. A poet called Smedley joined them, to be massaged in mildness by a nymph, called Merdamente. She whispered to him all the intricacies that he had ever hoped to find said to him underneath the waves of Thames.

The poet bared his teeth and sniffed. He picked up a lamprey from the pan with silver tongs and blew softly on it a puff of cadaverous breath. The little fish cooled and the poet slurped the boneless body through a pair of pursed lips. A drop of butterfat slid down his chin to solidify yellowly at the tip. He glanced at the cross of Christ on the wall above his table. Back to work.

"Sweet Thames, run softly, till I end my Song."

XXI

HOME. IRELAND. THE ship thumped into the soft decaying bulwark on the South Quay in Cork. Faint lights of houses up on the hill. Soft yellow. Outside the thick walls. Behind me I could see, by moonlight, the twin pillars of the port entrance. A light swung on the parapet of one of them. Soft air of Cork City. Midden-heaps infected the night breezes. The tang of Munster. Out there the Atlantic distance which those pillars emphasised. Out there.

My thoughts were on nothing. Blank misgiving – that was all. An excitement, too, a physical heightening. A coming "home", as I was recognising I was beginning to call this place.

The long journey to Cork. But tonight I would spend drinking. That was how to come home. Drink, blindness, the city's instinct.

XXII

M Y COMPANION WAS a long-haired Irishman whose English was good. Telling me a story about the old days, before "your good selves", the English, came.

"I'll tell you, sir, it was crazy. There was no law or regulation of any kind. Just sheer craziness. There was, no lie, there was a man walking the road one day and his wife was with him. She was a beauty. Bursting out of her blouse. And the spring of her walk a torment. But as he was going – I think it was to market or something like that, God knows – he met another man, a strange fellow who greeted him warmly and bade him the time of day.

"'There's a fine woman there you have,' said the stranger.

"'Well,' says the husband, 'I suppose she's not too bad.'

"You see, sir, he was the accommodating type. Always axed by a question.

"Anyway the stranger asked the husband if he would lend him his wife for an hour and a quarter. The husband was shocked. Something crawled in his head. 'Is this jealousy,' he asked. 'Why should I suspect?'

"'What for?' he asked.

"'Well, I wish to employ her in a certain business. That is all. No harm intended, no harm at all.'

"'No harm? Well,' (and as he said this every vein in his body cried out to him not to do what he was going to do, but he was trapped. Trapped, by accommodating). 'Well,' he said, 'I suppose that's all right then, as long as my wife has no objection. Do you object?' he asked her.

"'It is not for me to object. You must decide. That, husband, is your lordliness, which no one can share.'

"'Then go.'

"'Thank you. I will see you at the bend of the road above the river in an hour and a quarter.'

"And so they went, leaving the husband forlorn, hoping that the stranger had told the truth. He imagined them, in a copse, his wife on the ground, her eyes closed, giving small cries of pleasure as the stranger's penis surged in and out of her. He saw it glistening with her intimacy and his whole stomach ached with love and stress and misery. That was how it was.

"He wandered along the roadside just barely noticing

115

the blackbird cheeping on top of the chestnut, emitting great spurts of song, descants in the soft leaves.

"He came to the bend of the road. The time had surely elapsed by now. He saw them coming along a worn dirt-track. They were laughing. He could hear his wife's peals of bright mirth as the stranger entertained her with stories and jests. They strode along like young lovers. His pain brewed inside him. But it was his consent. His consent. He was a cuckold through accommodation.

"When they came up to him, his wife's hair was dishevelled, her face flushed, her skin relaxed and shining. She glowed with beauty and satisfaction. Forever now they should be apart.

"'What did you do?' he asked the stranger.

"'Oh, nothing,' the other replied, looking at the woman and laughing. 'A thing of nothing, the merest thing you can think of. Can you see any change? Nothing. And thank you for being so – what shall I say – accommodating. Good morning. And, Mistress Cunny, good morning to you.'

"That is the story. And, you know, if it weren't that my own little mother was a woman, there's many other stories I could tell you about them. Women, that is. But that's all over now, thank God, since 'your good selves' came over here. Our women are now subdued."

"But how has our presence subdued your women? I do not follow."

"Oh well, it's simple. You have shown us that they are themselves the stranger. They are out there, when we thought that they were just like ourselves. They are terrors to our dreams now, but they no longer terrorise our lives. So we make them housewives, or try to, imitating the good example of the Undertakers, like yourselves."

I called for more wine and drank deeply. The rawness of the claret attacked my throat. I was going under. My companion was telling me of the old poetry of this country, what it did, and how useless it had been, but as he spoke I realised that he himself had been such a poet and I think the word he used for his craft, in translation, was "deep-operator".

"I tell you, Master Spenser, it was crazy. The stanza was a box enmeshed with rhyme and assonance. My old teacher used to say it was a box for listening and seeing, and he said if you looked at a stanza, or better, held one in your head, you could hear the rustle of the leaves, and smell summer, and see people going by over a long road into the mountains. The box crackled with a silent intangible wind coming from out of those mountains. Technique, he said, was the darkness crackling through. In those stanzas that he taught us, in grey unhappy laboriousness, he said we would be fully ourselves. No other way. No other operation for it. That was it. Should this go, he would say (and at this his eyes would water, looking at the knob of his clasped hands), we would never again be ourselves. Lost souls without this transmission from the dark mountains.

"I never believed him all those long years; twelve it was, twelve years with the session in the stone tomb twice a week to compose a stupid verse on a rabbit or on a story from the Bible – marriage of Cana, that kind of stuff. And then one day I went into the stone room which was entirely dark, and it was there. The stones themselves laden with knowledge and order. In the dark I saw their structure. Fiery criss-crossings, chimings and assonances. I saw that that which was solid, silent, the stone, was in fact alive and crackling, ablaze with depth and activity. The crackle came straight from a dark mountain range into the stones. And I set a poem going in my head about a journey to a quiet place through bleak terrain. A woman holding a child to her breast, walking endlessly the hard roads, the child ill and she feeding it from her dry dugs, when they come upon a ruined cottage, with only part of its roof left. A ragged piece of cloth is stirred in the window and a tired face looks out. A man with deep blue eyes and a ragged beard. He is white with long suffering. He speaks to the woman, and asks her how the little one is. She replies that she is afraid it is going to die from lack of food, and that it is sore from dirt. The man at the window disappears into the house and comes out with a very fine and clean yard of linen, smelling sweet and fresh.

"'This will do,' he says, 'this will do. Let me help.' Together they change the little child into the comfortable linen. It falls asleep immediately in the warm cleanliness.

"'Your journey is nearly done,' says the man. 'Nearly done. Not much farther. Another hour and you'll be there.'

"'Where shall I be?'

"'You will be in the bright mountains of love where you will be fed and clothed and your breast will swell again with the purest milk.'

"'And why do you stay here?'

"'I am the watcher of the spirit. I tend those who need help along the last stretch of the journey and there are those I send astray into the deeper wilderness. But you go to the mountains of the light, where your child will be a man to bring you peace.'

"That was my first real poem. The stanzas assembled of themselves. They seemed composed of yellow light. They were afire with love. My teacher was pleased, but warned me that I might find it hard to sell.

"'A more modest undertaking would find more favour,' he said.

"But I've stopped all that trade now. Useless. I've gone into the wine importation business. Have another claret, poet. Let's get drunk in the name of memory, Mnemosyne; I remembering my only real poem, you remembering the England you seek to represent."

I must have looked at him sharply, though by now my senses were dulled.

"Oh yes, I know your work, and have heard of the masterpiece. Does she deserve it?"

"Who?"

"The Queen."

Misgiving, fear, mistrust. "Yes."

Later, drunk, I heard him saying through a haze of wine fumes: "You know, you and I – we can never be friends. We are too apart. And you try to remember too much. You are tricked by Mnemosyne. You cannot join us. And in any case we would not have you. We would make use of

119

you if you were weaker. We could extract some information from you, maybe, or use you to communicate some
false information to your superiors, but no, you are no use.
You are too difficult and stupid to belong with us, and
your memory is too conscientious to be of any use to that
lot in London, the Queen's ministers, those dark men who
breathe grey light in dim rooms. Their innards steel. In
the end they will kill you, have no doubt. They will kill you
either through neglect, if you have patience, or, if they
haven't, just simply kill you. A knife, poison, or the axe in
the back of the head some dark night."

That night I dreamt I was talking with Raleigh. The
blue eyes turned towards me often as we walked in a
garden beneath an old house. He told me he had plans to
live quietly and invited me to join him. We would live on
his estate in Ireland and he would try to create a free
country, under his mild authority. When he looked at me
his eyes were so kind.

"It is simple, Spenser, simple. We have enough money.
What more do we require, you and I. We can forget about
England. Take our women and live in peace. Watch the
children grow and forget about the grey wilderness in
London. Ireland is Arcadia, Edmund, a possibility which
we may realise. We English can tell ourselves the story of
the Italian idyll and make it real in Ireland. Why not?
What can stop us? The tired old Queen can go to hell. No
more the sweat in the armpits as we walk the long tiled
corridors, fearing them, fearing our weakness, afraid of
the illness that those places cause. Let us go. What is mine,
my friend, is yours. There is to be no more dying like this.

We go to live and when our death comes it comes as peace, no panic-stricken forays into the past to try to think of what it is we've done that we can say for ourselves at the end."

He stopped talking. I looked around the garden. It had changed. The sunlight had deepened; there was more colour. The green was enriched. Two men were playing tennis in a court. Their white stood out against the green hedgerows.

Again he spoke: "It is so easy; such a little thing. Why not? Why not take our chance now? It may not come again."

I seemed to feel the warmth of the day in my blood. What was there to be lost?

I awoke filled with joy. Soon, however, I realised how nauseous my stomach was, how my head felt tightened with pain.

XXIII

Youghal in east County Cork. I started going there regularly very soon after I returned to Kilcolman. Raleigh not often there, but I had another interest: my future wife, my dear Elizabeth, successor to Machabyas.

One day, having walked along the strand, we sat upon a headland looking out to sea. A quiet summer day, the water still and clear, the mackerel rippling into sudden flurries of activity as they ran after the shoals of sprat, devouring them. The air tingled with their hunting and my excitement.

"My dear one, Elizabeth. You have rescued me from the darkness of myself."

She hated that kind of talk. Still does. No time for it.

"Edmund, don't be so Puritan serious. When I saw you that day rounding the corner in Youghal, with your showy black hat, I thought – there goes a serious one. You looked so pale. John-o'-Dreams. A stumbler. In fact you did stumble as you came towards me. I saw you looking at my feet."

"I remember that day. The light hanging in the greyness of the afternoon. It seemed sharp. Things standing out more. Each movement of your body a confirmation of some minute glory."

I thought of the acres of ocean stretching between this small sea-port and the blazing colours of London; and I thought of Raleigh out there on the waters, in his ship, securing the large beam, the thick masts, the sails thundering into tautness as the wind changes, and I knew again that life was good.

XXIV

YOUGHAL, MOUTH OF the Blackwater. Black water. In the estuary is where I dreamed him, Raleigh, with his blue eyes. That is where he is chambered. And is where I must release him from. I flew out from the harbour, bird-like, moving over the water, no more than a foot above the surface. The light was dull and the sea calm. Diving beneath I saw great hulks, great red wrecks, monstrous congers as thick as my waist going in and out of gaps in the planking. I saw right down to bottom. It was as if the seabed itself had thrown out a green light illuminating the depth. The congers flash greenly by, white bellies startling for a moment. And there is the rock of some black ironstone, adamantine. I plummet down and come to its rough surface, covered in limpets and mussels. There is a rusted iron ring, sunk in the top, which I lift with difficulty. Below, a series of steps cut out of the stone, descending. A green light comes from below. I go down, and find myself in the chamber I have described already. Flaring torches on the walls, the floor covered with a soft dry seaweed and on a dias or bier a young girl, naked, her nipples dark in the greenish-blue light. This was Raleigh. A movement to the right. Lurching towards me a half-man half-woman in heavy dark clothing, a watery smile on its face. The skin pale and pocked with blackheads, oily. I drew my heavy sword and slashed wildly at it. I got it in the neck and blood spurted, covering its dark clothes. It still laughed.

The girl on the stone couch was breathing. Unbelievably, she broke into a faint song of forests that were misted, long days of sunlight, the dark fruit of the vine clammy and rich. The whey hermaphrodite staggered against the wall, bleeding profusely from head and neck. I struck once more, this time into the ribcage and felt the shock of iron hitting upon bone. The girl on the couch stirred and raised herself on one arm, the breasts acquiring greater fullness as she did, drooping slightly away from her body. There was a stink of blood. She spoke.

"Can you not leave that and come to me? All that you have known cannot extricate you now. You have struck in and you must proceed. My body is your engine for delight. What you can know now through me no one has ever known before. It will be light, a light throughout your whole system. There's no more dying then. No more. Come."

"I cannot," I replied. "If I go to you now I must die. That is what you ask. And I am not ready yet. I do not want to seek my death through impatience. Steady. I must be steady. It would be a great mistake to go along with the excitement that is moving now. A great mistake. I must be easy."

"To be easy is to miss so much," she said. "All the fire and success is opposite to that."

"No, I do not think so." And then she began to become male. The breasts shrank back, the body thickened. And beneath the light down at the mount of Venus a penis began to emerge. It was erect.

The eyes glittered blue.

"If I cannot excite you that way, then maybe this," he said. It was Raleigh.

"I cannot rescue you, Walter. I cannot. Even if I do what you ask you cannot be freed. Only I will be lost as well. You cannot be rescued. There is only one who rescues. Whatever sympathy I have for you (and it is great, though I could wish it greater) in the end there is nothing I can do for you. You are in your solitude."

A face glimmered in the dark. A bleak bearded face, a kindly face, but with the set air of satisfaction. An elaborate metal structure supported his jaw and impeded his speech somewhat.

"You see," the head said, "it is not possible for us to be happy. There is really no sense in trying for the solution to any of our mysteries in the hope that if we can find the key we can be released. There is, after all the analysis, the prospect of a life lived in grey composure. Do not speak to me of happiness. It is the condition of the inane or the lunatic. All we hope for is a steady focus, and a grim determination to pursue our fear to its hiding place. It is a kind of release, a relaxation to know that we need not always continue to strive so desperately after what has been promised us so faithfully. They did promise us so faithfully. My father said so. He said that I would be happy, that he and I would sit down together in a cool light and share our bread. But it is not so. The man died, and he never spoke to me. Never. He never turned to speak to me of normal things. So I grow more composed in this bleak metal harness on my jaw."

I spoke to Raleigh.

"There is release, Walter, there is. Coherence does present itself. There is joy. Give that up and we give everything up. All possibility of loving, even of action. The meanest movement springs from the certainty that all resides in joy."

Then that was all there was. I do not dream this dream any more. I had it some six months after my marriage to Elizabeth.

XXV

A FISH OF IRON is nosing through the dark waters. A yellow light comes from the interior. On the side of this iron fish a red cross, brightly, even harshly painted. Inside a grey-haired man, with smooth skin and a full beard. He has been sent underwater and he has been travelling there for many years. He is looking for a dark rock shelf, with a ring of iron set in the top. He is to have a meeting there with a young girl, whose eyes are of the sea, whose skin is green.

He will find her, under there. Sometimes in the long passages of the dark waters, navigating where he has never been before, he sits at an iron bench, bolted to the floor, writing notes about a poet who lived one time, who dreamed of a Queen, whose name was glory itself.